my sister's boyfriend

my sister's boyfriend

my sister's boyfriend

a novel by
Natty Soltesz

QUEERMOJO
A Rebel Satori Imprint
New Orleans

Published in the United States of America by
Queer Mojo
A Rebel Satori Imprint
www.rebelsatoripress.com

This is a work of fiction. Names, characters, places, and incidents
are the product of the author's imagination and are used fictitiously
and any resemblance to actual persons, living or dead, business
establishments, events, or locales is entirely coincidental. The
publisher does not have any control over and does not assume any
responsibility for author or third-party websites or their content.

Cover image by Danilo Lisik.

ISBN: 978-1-60864-167-3

my sister's boyfriend

my sister's boyfriend

1

My sister's boyfriend Joey. That's all he was to me before I met him, something my mom said to me on the phone: *Your sister's boyfriend, that Joey.*

Just a boyfriend in a string of boyfriends, going back from when we were kids. I remember her kissing Travis Meyer on the monkey bars of our elementary school playground. At a junior-high pool party, nuzzling a boy on a towel in the grass, holding hands with him as they strode to the water and dove in. I was off to the side (as I often was) watching Ryan Cowley strip down to his surprisingly hairy and manly chest and wondering what it would feel like to nuzzle somebody of my own.

It was awkward, those parties. By high school, it didn't happen as much. My sister and I had found our respective crowds—her with the jocks and popular kids, me with the druggies and artists.

I guess I noticed her boyfriends, but they usually didn't interest me. There was Matt, the boy whose parents owned the lumber store off the highway. And Christopher, whose dream in life was to become a lawyer. She always liked those straight-laced, bourgeois types. She seemed to be auditioning husbands rather than, like, actually enjoying herself.

But with Joey, it was different. For both of us.

I'd just got home the night before—Groom, Pennsylvania, the town I grew up in, the town where my mom and sister still lived. I'd graduated from college a week before with a degree in anthropology, and I was in Groom for the summer to save some money before I moved to New York City. At least that's what I was telling myself.

Trisha cornered me right before we sat down to eat. "Can you help me and Joey move a bed into my new place?" she said. "Joey's gonna help, but it's a pretty big bed."

"Why are you whispering?" I said.

She glanced around the corner where Mom was puttering around in the kitchen, talking to herself. "I'm not," she said. "I'm *not*," she said louder. "But don't tell Mom," she said, whispering.

"C'mon, Trish. I just got home."

"Yeah, and you had all day today to lay around. What'd you even do?"

"I got high and watched the Brady Bunch," I said and leveled her gaze. "Why can't I tell Mom?"

"She just...she's all weird about Joey. She annoys the hell out of me when she talks about him, so just don't bring him up, okay?"

"Okay."

"And help me move the bed?"

"Sure."

Now we were driving to her new place, which was on Falling Run Road, one of my favorite roads to drive out and

2

get stoned on. It's a country road, a mile or so out of town and past a couple farms. It starts on top of a hill then descends into deep forest, twisting and turning through the hollow. There are only a few houses along the lane, and most of them sit up from the road.

Trish looked at me from the driver's seat. "Look, I just didn't want Mom to ask too many questions at dinner," she said. "Joey's living with me. I mean, we're moving in together."

"You think she'll care?" I said.

"I don't know. I don't care. It's none of her business anyway," she said, whipping too hard around a curve in the road. I grabbed the "oh shit" handle and righted myself.

"She'll probably start asking you when you're gonna get married."

"You say that as if she's not doing it already," Trish said and clenched her teeth.

"Are you going to get married?"

"Are you going to get your shit together?" Trish said, grinning at me.

"I feel like my shit is pretty well together. I did just graduate from college, after all."

"With a degree in archeology."

"Anthropology, moron."

"That seems useful."

"I'm moving to New York." I looked out the window.

"Yeah, what is that all about, anyway? Why didn't you just major in art if you're going to be an artist?"

"I'm more well-rounded this way," I said, hating her. The fact was that I didn't know why I'd majored in anthropology.

3

I'd known it was a useless major, but it interested me.

"You should just get a job at the bank. We have benefits, at least," she said. Trisha had worked at the local bank for the past two years.

"I'm healthy enough."

"Yeah, well, we'll see how healthy you are after you've been living with Mom for a few weeks."

"She never used to be this bad when Dad was around."

Trish didn't say anything, but she didn't have to. Dad's death eight years ago had changed all of us.

We pulled up to her house. The driveway was on a steep incline. Then we turned off into a flat area, and there was the house, cute and stout and sided in wood. It was like a perfect forest bungalow, a double-sized cozy cabin in the woods.

I asked, "How'd you find this place?"

"Right?" Trish said, looking at me admiring it. "*Pennysaver.* Wait till you see. It's all leveled out in the back, and there's a yard and a garden. Well, a space for one." She put the emergency brake on and we got out of the car.

The place was perfect. The kitchen was done up like a fairy-tale cottage with wood cabinets all blond and lacquered, with little heart cutouts on the front of them. The bathroom was tiled in pink and blue. The backyard was idyllic, hidden from the road by the house in front and right at the bottom of a cascade of forest.

"Where's the bedroom?" I said, but Trisha was walking back outside.

"It's…there," she said. "Hold on. Joey's here."

I heard car wheels on a gravel road and followed her

outside. There was an old maroon-colored Cadillac ambling up the driveway.

"Nice car," I said to Trish. She shot me a look I couldn't quite place, but I chalked it up to the fact that she didn't have much of an appreciation for antiques. The car was the shit, though, a real land yacht—a rambling thing that looked like it could comfortably host a party of four in the back seat. A mattress was strapped to the top. And driving it was Joey.

He parked and got out. He regarded me. I guess I did the same. He reminded me of somebody who I couldn't quite place, so I guess I looked at him harder and he looked right back. He was fair-haired with a light mustache, and his head was shaved to the nub. His skin was pale, and he had a trim but solid body, with muscles that showed well in his wife beater.

It was that look—an instant connection, whatever it was, whatever it meant. Trish gave him a quick kiss on the cheek. He glanced at her passing face, then right back at me.

Trisha pulled at the ropes that were tying down the mattress. "Do you think we can get it to the front door? Where's the headboard—in the back?"

"Yeah, yeah," Joey said to her. "Is this your brother?"

Trisha was already going around to the back, opening the trunk and stuffing her head inside. "Where's the screws for everything? Are they in the glove box?" she said.

Meanwhile, Joey went up to me and held out his hand.

I shook it. "I'm Nate," I said. "You're Joey."

"Nice to meet you," he said. Looked in my eyes, smiled. Did our hands linger longer than normal? Joey looked back at my sister, who had one corner of the mattress untethered and

5

was trying to lift it off the car. We watched her fumble with it until she finally looked at us.

"It's nice of my sister to introduce us," I said.

"Are you gonna help me with this thing or what?" she said.

We took the mattress into the house, Joey and me. And, you know, he was straining and his muscles were working and it looked quite nice, though I wasn't particularly dwelling on the fact of his hotness, just noticing, tagging and releasing it. Or maybe I was just telling myself that because I didn't want to think I was flirting with him. I wasn't *trying* to flirt with him, but I don't know. My ex-boyfriend, Eric, told me once that the very thing that made me attractive was that I was so blissfully unaware of how attractive I was.

By the time we got inside, I realized I still didn't know where the bedroom was.

"It's here?" I said to Joey when we got to the door that seemed right. Joey nodded, and I managed to open the door while hefting the mattress in my other hand.

My sister's new bedroom was unlike any bedroom she'd had before. There were dark red curtains on the windows and, like, bolts of silk hanging from the walls. I swear her bedside lamp had something that looked like a lace teddy covering the shade, and when Joey flipped it on, it bathed the room in lurid red light. Her last apartment had been spartan—she didn't even have magnets on her fridge. Now, she was handily achieving the French brothel effect.

6

We set the mattress on the frame. All that was left was to attach the headboard, throw some sheets on it—silk, no doubt—light some vanilla-scented candles, and bone away.

"Damn, it's hot," Joey said. He stripped off his shirt, wiped his face with it. Curious. He was gorgeous in this trashy way, which is terrible to say, I know, but it wasn't a judgment. He was blue collar all the way. Mom had already told me that he worked construction, that his parents lived in a trailer up the highway.

Trish came up and stood in the doorway. In her hands was a sandwich baggie of nuts and screws, which she'd no doubt bagged up herself. The bag even had a strip of Scotch tape to keep it closed.

"How's it look?" she said.

"Can't you see it?" I said.

"Not really from back here," she said. The room was big, and the bed was against the far wall, but still.

"I would suggest walking into the bedroom to get a closer look," I said. She rolled her eyes and did it.

And after I'd helped Joey screw in the headboard—he'd been writhing around on the floor in the dust and dirt so that sweat and swipes of dirt were on the alabaster skin of his arms—we stood at the foot of the bed and admired our handiwork. Our bodies were close together. I could smell him: sweaty, but wearing deodorant or some mild cologne. Trisha was in the kitchen, slamming cupboard doors.

He looked at me. "Wanna take a nap?" he said in this quiet voice, smiling, and I laughed like it was funny.

7

2

Was I bored? It was two days into my summer vacation, if I was having a summer vacation, now that I was supposedly an adult.

I was bored. I was getting sick of my family, too. Trish came over for dinner at Mom's again the next night. We sat around the table. Trish talked, and Mom talked, and I didn't talk; our normal modes were all accounted for. I'm an inward type of person, it should be said, but it should also be said that my mom and sister suck the air like vacuums until there's nothing left to breath.

There was a pause in the conversation. "So, Nate," my mom began, and I braced myself because nothing good has ever come after she addresses me in that way. "Trish was saying just yesterday that one of the girls she works with might be quitting."

"Might be, no—she quit today," Trish said. She looked at Mom, assessed that Mom was going in for the kill, and leaned back in her chair.

"Oh, is that so? Even better," Mom said.

"Why?" I said.

"Well, it could be a good opportunity for you. I mean, here you are, and I know you have plans to move to the big city"— she said the words "big city" like they were made of all-too-precious metal—"but in the meantime, it wouldn't be a bad idea to get a job, you know. Get some real-world experience."

Trish gnawed on a dinner roll and watched me.

"I'm going to get a job," I said. "When did I ever say I wasn't getting one? I need to save money. That's the whole point. Languish here for the summer...."

"Languish!" Mom said, rolling her eyes.

I ignored her. "And save up enough to move by September. But I don't want to work at the bank." In my head, I thought, *I'd rather die than waste one hour of my life in an office job with my sister.*

"Why not?" Trish said.

"Yes, explain that," Mom said. The wolves were circling. I just shrugged—a retreat.

"You'll have loans to start paying back soon," Mom said. "Will you be able to save as much as you want?"

"Yeah, and don't you think it's lame to freeload off of Mom for a whole summer?" Trish said. I glared at her.

"That's not what this is about," Mom said, waving her hand at both of us. "He should do something responsible, like you do, Trish. Something grounded...." They were starting up again, vacuums in perpetual motion, only now they were yawning on about me.

"Oh shit," I said and looked at my phone. "I totally forgot." I got up from the table and pretended like I was scrambling.

"What? What is it?" Mom said. Trish couldn't help but be amused. She knew this tactic all too well. She'd taught it to me after all.

"It's Nick. We were supposed to go out and, uh, meet. To help his brother."

"Isn't Nick in Ocean City?" Trish said.

My eyes shot daggers her way. "He just got back," I said.

"Oh."

"You really have to go right now, Nate?" Mom said.

"Thanks for dinner," I said and kissed her on the forehead. "Don't wait up for me."

"Well, if you come home as late as you did last night, make sure you lock the door behind you. And if you use the bathroom, please try to go in quietly. You woke me last night, and it took me over half an hour to fall back asleep."

"Will do, Mom," I said.

"Tell Nick I said hey," Trish said.

I had one foot out of the kitchen, but I turned back to her. "He has a girlfriend. And you've got Joey. Is he spending the night at your house again tonight?" I said.

"He *what*—" Mom said, and I got the fuck out of there, properly avenged, but still seething at how readily Trish had thrown me under the bus. I hate her sometimes, but I've never hated her as much as when she briefly dated my best friend Nick in high school, and she knows it.

I really did have plans with Nick, but they weren't for a couple of hours. In the meantime, I had a joint tucked into the pocket of the flannel shirt I was wearing.

I walked out of the house. The sun was low in the sky, taking on that long-shadow syrupy glow that it does late in the day in the summer. I felt good—good to have escaped, good to be walking in my hometown.

Groom, Pennsylvania. There's something about being in the place where you grew up, especially a small town where you know every road and back alley, every crevice of it a part of you.

I needed matches, so I walked up to Sheetz and picked up a pack. Then I walked down the tracks. The weeds were high in the railroad yard, and the sun illuminated the pollen and bugs floating in the air. I walked along the tracks until I was out of town, then I turned into a clearing in the woods just off the tracks and lit up.

The smoke from the joint made lazy loops in the sunlight. It was this, this town, this feeling. I wanted to do this with my life—depict it, what I felt inside, try to articulate it. I didn't care about anthropology or humans in general. I'd already been locked into my major when I realized that what I really wanted to do with my life was art.

When he was young, my dad—me and Trisha's dad—wrote this book that is kind of famous called *The Martian Underground*. It's about a woman who's seduced by a Martian disguised as a human. The Martians had spent decades building this gigantic, secret underground city on Earth. They take humans there and use them as slave labor. The woman is the hero.

It's a weird book, but it has a following. There's a bunch of stuff about it online. I've read it a couple of times, but not since I was a kid. My sister hates it.

I just knew that if he could do something like that, something that was a legacy, then I had the potential to do the same thing.

I'd been drawing since I was a little kid, but even when I

had won a state award in high school for a drawing that I did in my tenth grade art class, I never took it seriously. My mom never encouraged it.

I could hardly stand to think of myself like that: an *artiste*. But that was what I had to be.

New York City. That was where I wanted to get to, where I was going to get to, where I was going to do it. I didn't know how—I didn't really know anybody there—but it was important, mostly because I didn't have any other plan. I had some money saved up. Not a ton.

Fuck. I needed a job.

But in the meantime, I needed to use this summer to kick some ass and make some art, and I resolved to do that then and there.

Of course, that's not how it wound up working out.

I met Nick at a bar in town called the Silver-Tongued Devil. I'm not much of a drinker, and the bars in my hometown scare me, but I was feeling adventurous. They had Mardi Gras streamers everywhere, I guess cause they liked the colors. Three girls were kicking up their heels on a dance floor about the square footage of a refrigerator box, and five guys sat along the bar and turned back occasionally to look at them.

I sidled up to the bar and ordered a beer. Nick came in a few minutes later. He was still a sexy guy—tall, dark, and handsome, a bit thicker around the middle than he'd been in high school. His tan looked good on him. We slapped palms

12

and he sat down.

"Just got back from the beach, yeah?" I said.

"Yeah," he said. Ordered a shot and a beer. I watched him down the shot. It made me feel lonely, like I should be doing one, too. But things were different between us. They'd never really been the same after he dated Trish.

"Who'd you go with?"

"Amy's family." Amy was his girlfriend, I reminded myself. They lived together. "They got a house ocean side. It was nice." Nick is a man of few words. It could be why we became friends. We're both the quiet type. "I got a tan," he said.

"I noticed," I said and sucked on my beer. Nick turned around to watch the girls dance, turned back to me.

I took another gulp of beer. "Did you draw anything down there?" I said.

"No. I haven't been drawing in a while, really."

"You're working?"

"Yeah, I just got a new job. At the sewing machine factory?"

"Oh yeah. I've always wondered about that place." It's a factory on the edge of town, a big rectangular building, with tons of little windows. It's just down the tracks from my mom's house. "I used to imagine I could hear it at night from my bedroom window," I continued. Nick regarded me. "It was probably just the sound of trucks on the highway."

"It's an okay job," Nick said. "Congratulations, by the way. On graduating."

"Thanks, man," I said and started to feel really awkward, like I'd succeeded where he failed.

"Are you just here for the summer?"

"Yeah. I'm planning to move to New York," I said.

"Right on," Nick said, and I instantly felt stupid for saying that I was going to *New York City*, like I was rubbing it in his face.

We kept up the conversation, superficial as it was. He had a weed hookup. I told him I'd probably need to use that sooner than later. We didn't order a second beer.

Nick and I, we'd once been close. Closer than close, in some important ways. We had our sophomore art class together. We realized that we both liked to draw, and then our junior year, we started hanging out and drawing together, which was nice because we didn't have to talk a lot. But we would end up talking, as if working side by side released some social tension and anxiety. That was how I ended up telling Nick that I was gay.

"I figured you were into something different. You're just that kind of guy," he said, and that was that.

Nick was on the football team his first two years of high school and was good at it, but then he tore a tendon in his foot and couldn't play anymore. So, we'd hang out in his attic bedroom, or sometimes we'd drive around and see movies. Once I came out to Nick, he found it easier to talk to me about girls, with whom he'd never had a lot of luck. Soon he was talking to me about nothing *but* girls. And I was as horny as he was, but for guys. The more we hung out, the more I began to realize that it was mainly *him* I was horny for.

14

Once he told me that he had a big dick, that guys on the football team had called him "Tripod." That stuck, but the idea of messing around with him was too complex and messy to ponder.

Until it happened. It was the spring of our junior year, and we were up in Nick's attic, drawing like we usually were, him at his desk and me in the beanbag chair at his feet, music on the stereo. I was doing these little pop art pieces, drawing things around Nick's room like his tube of deodorant and his bottle of eye drops.

"Courtney Senick doesn't wear a sports bra," he said, eyes on his drawing. "I see her in gym class, bouncing around. It's criminal. I start getting hard while we're playing volleyball. I had to go to the bathroom the other day."

"Did you jack off in the stall?" I said.

"Yeah." Nick laughed.

I laughed with him. "I've jacked off in the faculty restroom on the second floor. The one that locks," I said.

"I jack off so much," Nick said. He'd had a girlfriend his sophomore year, so he wasn't a virgin, unlike me. What's more, he'd had sex a bunch with his ex—or at least a few times— and she'd sucked his dick. I never plied him for details cause it made me jealous, like he was part of the non-virgin club.

"Me, too," I said. We kept drawing, but the weirdest feeling came over the room: I was getting turned on, and it felt like I could tell he was getting turned on, too.

"I have porn," he said finally.

"Like, movies?" I said.

"Magazines. They were my brother's. I found them in his

closet."

"What are they like?" I said, and Nick laughed.

"You might like them," he said. "They have big dicks in them."

"Where are they?"

Nick got up and his dick was tenting out the front of his shorts. My heart started beating like crazy. He rooted around in the bottom drawer of his dresser and came out with a couple of magazines, handing two to me and taking one back to his bed. He laid back and flipped through it. I did the same.

They were hardcore. Most of the pictorials were of two guys fucking one girl, which was a delightful surprise. "You're right," I said. "I do like them."

"I thought you might. Are the dicks big enough for you?" he said.

"Some of them," I said. I was so hard in my jeans. "Like, look at this guy's." I held up the magazine, and Nick leaned over to see.

"That's not *that* big," he said.

"You've seen bigger?" I said.

"I like her," he said, holding a magazine for me to see. I nodded noncommittally. "Anyway, my dick's bigger than that one." Nick's erection was totally apparent, lying like a pipe in his lap, and I wasn't trying to hide mine either.

"Is it?" I looked right at his lap.

He followed my gaze. "Yeah," he said. He pulled the waistband of his shorts down. He wasn't wearing underwear. "See?" His hard dick lolled up and out and hung there like a dog's tongue. It was huge.

"Wow," I said.

"I told you," he said, laughing a little. He tucked it back inside his shorts.

"Mine isn't anywhere near that."

"Lemme see."

I stood up. The metal chinked as I unbuckled my belt, then I held out my cock.

"It's a nice cock," Nick said diplomatically.

"Thanks. Yours is really nice."

Nick stood and took out his cock again. "We're both horny," he said.

"Yeah."

"Would it be weird if we did something right now?" he said. I answered by reaching out and taking his cock in the palm of my hand, the first cock I'd ever touched besides my own. It felt so good, heavy and hot. Nick took hold of mine, and we stood there for a minute, stroking each other. Nick looked in my eyes. "Just this one time, okay?" he said. I nodded, as if I could have said no. I would have agreed to murder if it meant we could keep doing what we were doing.

Nick knelt. He gulped, then he put his lips around my cock. He sucked on the head. He took it deeper, slathering his tongue along the underside as he got it part of the way into his throat. It was toothy, I remember, not that I cared. He gave it a few passes, then stood up and wiped his mouth.

"Sorry if that was bad. I never did it before."

"I never have either."

"I'll help you," he said, and he did. I started on my knees. That big hairy dick was right in my face. I took a deep breath and kissed it, right on the head. There was a drop of pre-come there and it smeared on my lips. I licked it and the taste, plus the smell of his crotch, was all so different, but good. I sucked on the head, and it was like sucking on a plum. I chanced taking it past my throat.

"Watch your teeth," Nick said in a kind way. "Here." He lay back on the bed. I got in between his legs and we found a comfortable position. I went back to work, curling my lips around my teeth and managing to take more of him in. "That's good," Nick said after a few passes of my mouth. "Oh damn, that's good." I got a rhythm going. It was hard work, actually. I've never been able to breathe through my nose too well, so I kept backing off to catch my breath. Nick was a cool customer, totally into whatever I was doing, just laying back and enjoying himself.

"Lick my balls," he instructed.

I lapped them up and Nick groaned. I could tell he was tentative about telling me what to do. It was not in his personality to be commanding. But maybe it got easier for him when he saw how much it turned me on.

"Lick real slow up the shaft and kind of suck on the head like you were doing earlier. God, fuck, yes." He whispered all of this, and I knew his family was downstairs with no idea of what we were doing. "Suck it as deep as you can." I managed to get the whole thing down my throat that first time. What can I say? I'm a natural. I choked after a few seconds, but I still did it. "Holy fuck. I can't believe you can do that."

"I can't believe it either."

"It felt amazing. Do it again." I did it again. I ran my hands

18

up under Nick's shirt, feeling his hairy stomach, his softly muscled tits. I felt his thighs, too, which were thick and strong. "Suck my balls some more before I...oh fuck, I'm gonna come. Take it all the way." I took it down deep and came back up, and he started shooting in my mouth. I'd been uncertain as to where I wanted him to come up to that point, but it happened, so I went with it. I even swallowed. It was pretty strange, but not bad.

Nick thanked me profusely, like he felt guilty for taking advantage of me. "That was a seriously amazing blowjob," he said.

I felt proud, and even though I hadn't gotten off, I had jack-off material for the rest of my life.

But it wasn't just that one time. We started doing it every time we hung out. Nick still got guilty afterward. He apologized for not sucking me again after that first time.

"It's okay. I get off on getting you off," I said.

"I know I'm not gay. You just give great head," he said.

The thing was, I believed him. Our friendship didn't change in any negative way. We were still buddies. We got together as much as we ever did, but we had this secret sex life.

After a few weeks, though, I found myself just wanting it more and feeling weird when he would have plans other than hanging out with me.

Then one night right before the end of the school year, we were in his room, drawing quietly, which was normal, but I had this sense that something had changed. Things felt tense.

"Wanna look at porn?" I finally said, which was also pretty normal, except Nick usually brought it up, and brought it up a lot sooner than I had.

"Nah," he said, and my heart sank. But it hadn't throttled through the earth's crust. Not yet.

"What's up?" I said.

"I think we might need to take a break," he said, glancing at me, pen still in hand, scratching away at his drawing pad.

"Any reason?"

"You know that party at Todd's this past weekend?"

"No," I said.

"Well, there was one," he said. "Your sister was there."

"Okay," I said, but my heart was beginning its rapid descent.

"We kinda hooked up."

That sinking feeling became nausea. "Hooked up?" I asked.

"Yeah, we made out. We ended up fooling around."

I put down my drawing and stared at the open window. It was dark outside. The tree branches had fresh leaves on them and the sodium streetlight gave it all a sickly glow.

"Are you upset?"

I didn't say anything.

"I'm sorry."

I just got up and left. Nick let me go, which made it even worse.

"I'm hanging out with Nick tonight," Trisha said the next day. "I like him."

"Good for you," I said.

20

"What, are you mad?"

"No," I said and steeled myself. I would not, could not, reveal how torn up I was inside, partly because I wasn't out to her (I didn't come out to my family until I went to college), and partly because I was embarrassed that I'd fallen into something with a straight guy, and a straight guy who liked my sister, no less.

I walked around a lot that summer. It was like the only thing I knew how to do. The worst thing about it was that there wasn't anybody to blame. Nobody had any loyalty to me or reason to think of me. I had no doubt that Nick and Trish were going to live happily ever after and I wanted to kill both of them, but that was exclusively my problem.

It was something that ended before it really even started. Trish dumped him, apparently. By then it seemed clear that Nick had betrayed me more than my sister had. No matter that our relationship was avowedly just a friendship, we'd both known it was a little bit more. But I'd expended so much mental energy on it that when Trish told me it ended, I couldn't muster any *schaudenfreude*.

Nick and I made amends a few weeks into our senior year, but things were never really the same.

Did Trish know that Nick and I had been more than friends? She never let on, but over the years, she would mention seeing him around town, and I swear she did it just to needle me.

3

"So, you helped Trisha move some things the other day," Mom said to me the next day. We sat across from one another at the kitchen table, finishing our dinner.

"Yeah," I said cautiously.

"Did you meet that Joey?"

"Why do you always call him *that* Joey?"

"You know what I mean. Joey. The construction worker."

"Yeah, I met him. He seems fine. Do you have a problem with him?"

"No, of course not," Mom said. "You know his parents live in the Morewood trailer park."

"Yeah, you've mentioned that."

"I don't know his parents. They don't go to church."

"They must be Satanists."

"Oh, don't say that."

"I'm joking."

"Well, you never know these days."

"You really think they might be Satanists?"

"No! All I *said* was that they didn't go to church."

I washed the dishes after dinner like a good son and then I got out of that house. I had a joint in my pocket, but I didn't wait until I was out of sight of the house. I just lit it up on the sidewalk, and by the time I'd circled the block, I'd smoked it to the nub and burned my fingers.

It didn't help. The days were passing. I still didn't have a job and I certainly didn't have any friends. Granted, I hadn't had high hopes for rekindling my relationship with Nick, but knowing I'd be stuck in Groom for at least a whole summer made me want to have *somebody* to hang out with. And now that we'd met up and things had been so awkward, I didn't even have hope for that. All I had was my sister and my mom.

And Joey, a voice in my head said, but I let that pass. It was too dangerous a thought, and it didn't have any basis in reality yet.

The one thing I *was* doing was catering to my mom. She was having some issues with her back. She had me drive her to her doctor's appointments, and get groceries, and enact any other number of demands that she could come up with. Sometimes I felt like I was atoning for going away to college for four years.

I coped with a steady intake of marijuana. If she wasn't home, I'd smoke on the rotting sun porch in the back of the house, which was piled with old stuff like my green plastic sled. One window had a pie-slice chunk of glass broken out of the corner, just like it'd been when I was a kid. The whole house was like that, a relic or shrine to my childhood.

One day I bought a bunch of food for the house, thinking she would appreciate it. She looked through the cupboards and the fridge at the stuff I bought and said, "What is this? What am I supposed to do with this?" I'd been stoned when I went to the store and, really, I'd bought a pile of pretty random stuff, like a box of cake mix, but no eggs, and a gigantic watermelon that barely fit in the fridge.

Now here I was, stoned again, and not even happily stoned. I wandered around until it was dark then went home.

The lights were on in the living room. When I walked in, Mom was sitting on the sofa, back erect, staring at me.

"Hi," I said. I was pretty stoned, and the way she looked at me was unnerving.

"I found your marijuana," she said.

My stomach sank to my balls. In front of her was my backpack, and inside, presumably, was a plastic baggy containing the dwindling contents of the ounce I'd bought off my ex-boyfriend Eric before I left Pittsburgh.

I took a deep breath. "Why were you going through my bag?"

"It doesn't matter," she said. The instant, crushing guilt I felt over disappointing my mother was beginning to dissipate.

"It sort of does," I said.

"This is my house, isn't it?"

"It's kind of *our* house, and that's *definitely* my bag."

"Don't avoid the subject."

"What do you want me to say? Yes, I smoke pot. I've been smoking it since I was in high school. I figured Trisha would've told you," I said, knowing full well that she never would— partly to protect me, but mostly to protect Mom, who didn't seem to know the difference between marijuana and heroin.

"Well, she didn't. I had my suspicions, and that's why I was going through your bag."

"You could've just asked. I would've told you."

"Really?"

"Probably," I said. "What do you want me to say?"

"That you won't bring drugs into my house again."

"Did you...," I said and looked into my bag.

24

Mom shifted in her seat, made herself impossibly more erect.

I asked, "What did you do with it?"

"I flushed it down the toilet."

"You *what*?" Now the anger came rushing in. Anger at her, anger at myself for thinking that living with my mom in my hometown for a summer would be a good idea. I grabbed my bag off the table and zipped it up. I headed for the door.

"Where are you going?"

"I'm going to stay with Trish tonight. And maybe for a little while."

"Oh, for heaven's sake. Just because I threw out your drugs."

"Look, I'm just...I need a change of scenery for a few days. That's all."

"Who's going to take me to the doctor's on Tuesday?"

"Jesus Christ, Mom. I'll just be at Trish's. Call me if you need me."

"I hope I'll be able to get a hold of you...," she was saying, but I was done. I rolled my eyes as I headed out.

Trish was not exactly happy to see me.

"What'd you do?" she asked as soon as she opened the door and saw me there on the stoop, bags in hand.

"Hi," I said and stepped around her. I plopped my bags down on the kitchen floor and Trish sighed, knowing what I was going to ask and resigned to it. "She's driving me crazy, Trish. She found my weed and threw it out." I sat down at the kitchen table.

"What a tragedy," she said, sitting across from me.

"Can I please just hide out here for a little while?"

"Like how long?"

"I don't know...the rest of the week?"

"Are you serious?"

"C'mon. I'll just crash on the couch. I won't intrude on your...love nest or whatever it is," I said, motioning to her bedroom.

"Gross," she said, shooting me a look.

"Your bedroom looks like a bordello, Trish."

She shrugged. "Joey likes it."

"I believe you."

"All right, but just for a couple days," she said.

"I need to get high," I said. Trish rolled her eyes at me. "You don't smoke weed anymore?" I said.

"No, pothead. The bank tests me. Joey does, though. I'm sure he'll be excited to have someone to sit around and get stoned with."

A thrill shot through me. Me and Joey, getting stoned...who knew what might happen?

"Do you think he'll be bothered that I'm here?"

Trish shrugged. "He works nights, so you'll probably see more of him than I do," she said.

"Where'd you meet him, anyway?"

"At a bar. The Roadhouse on Route 217."

"So, what's he all about? He just works construction?"

"Yeah, and he makes stuff. He has a woodworking shop with his dad. He's really good at it."

"Oh. So you have, like, ambitions for him?"

Trish wrinkled her nose at me. "It's not like that. We're in love."

"Wow. I don't think I've ever heard you say that before."

"I don't know that I've ever been in it before."

There was a pause while I let this information sink in.

Trisha said, "Anyway, don't say anything to Mom. I'm still figuring out how to tell her."

"I'm not going to. I already told you that. Why would I?"

"I don't know what you guys talk about."

"The same shit we talk about at dinner. How she's fighting with Donna, the current state of her hypochondria, the consistency of her bowel movements...."

Trisha laughed. I loved that I could make her laugh. I guess when we were growing up, Trisha got pegged as the uptight one. Especially after Dad died and she had to take the helm when Mom couldn't deal.

"She wants to know when I'm getting a job," I continued.

"When *are* you getting a job?"

"Christ, I don't know. Can't I just relax for a few days? I did just graduate from college, and it's only been...uh.... Oh fuck. Has it really been two weeks since I got back?"

"See?" Trisha said, sitting back in her chair. "This place is sucking you in."

"I need a job. Damn."

"Go to some restaurants. Wait tables."

"I hated doing that in college. Should I apply at the bank?" I said, feeling desperate.

"You don't want to work at the bank," Trisha said, and it wasn't so much a value judgment on me as something we both knew and accepted about ourselves: She was the one who took

27

the safe, responsible route, and I was the one who drifted.

◆

I got up early the next morning and just started walking. I ended up alongside the highway, and as soon as I saw the porn store, I knew.

I'd never been inside the place, but I'd known about it since I was a kid. The sign outside said ADULT in black letters on a yellow background. It had seemed so forbidden, and when we'd drive past it, Mom would honk her horn at the people going inside, just to shame them.

Now, I went inside. It was brightly lit, with rows of shelves: dildos, whips, and tons of DVDs. A man stood at the counter, older but handsome. He smiled at me and my gaydar went off. I'd seen him around town before.

His name was Randy, and when I told him I was looking for a job, he smiled and handed me an application. I filled it out on the counter, handed it to him. He looked it over. He asked me my situation and I told him: a graduate, probably just there for the summer, desperate for work. He nodded.

"It's not a bad job," he said. "Mostly, you'll be ringing people up for the coupons to go in the back. And you'll be cleaning the booths when you work the night shift."

"The booths?"

"Yeah," he said, motioning to the back of the store. There was a doorway. Inside it was a lit-up marquee filled with DVD covers. Beyond that was seemingly endless darkness.

"The booths back there," Randy said. "Some call it the Jack

Shack, but you didn't hear that from me."

"Oh," I said. "Oh," I said again, this time thinking of what my job was really going to entail.

"It's not that bad," Randy said. "Or maybe I'm just used to it."

"So, people jack off back there," I said.

"And more. But we don't talk about that." He reached behind the counter and pulled out a pair of industrial-strength green rubber gloves. "Any other questions?"

"I guess not," I said, looking at the gloves. Success as an artist never seemed so far away.

"Great. Come in tomorrow and we'll fill out paperwork. You'll probably get your first shift this weekend, maybe sooner. You're lucky. The night girl just quit."

"I do feel lucky," I said, relief coming over me. I had a job.

"Well, you are working at a porn store, remember."

"Have you worked here long?"

"I own the dump. And yes."

I celebrated my good fortune by calling up Nick. Thankfully, he answered and had weed to spare. I stopped by his house. His girlfriend was there. I'd never met her before. She was nice, and the visit wasn't entirely awkward, but it wasn't substantial either. I basically bought my bag and went on my way.

Trisha was home when I got back.

"I got a job at the porno store," I said.

"Oh, for God's sake," she said. "Mom's gonna love that."

We watched *Law & Order: SVU* until she went to bed. I crashed on the couch and woke up to Joey coming in the door.

I had an erection. Not because of him, but because I'd been asleep and it had just popped up. I pretended to stay asleep, but glanced at the clock. It was 2:00 a.m.

He walked behind the sofa and I sensed him observing me. He went into the bedroom. I listened to him murmuring with Trish. I started to drift off again when he came out of the bedroom. I looked at him.

"Hey," he said.

"Hey."

He went into the kitchen and got something out of the fridge. Then he came back into the living room and sat in the easy chair, which was close to my feet. I heard him crack open a can and take a fizzy gulp. My boner was going down and I had to pee, so I got up and took a piss in the bathroom. When I got back, Joey had turned on the TV. He wore silver athletic shorts, the silky ones that show off a guy's cock when he's freeballing, not that I could see much in the shifting blue light of the TV. He wore a wifebeater and had a gold chain around his neck.

I sat up on the couch, resigned to being awake until Joey decided to go to bed. Such are the options of one crashing on a couch.

"Want a beer?" he said, smiling at me and holding up his can. "There's more in the fridge."

"Yeah, I guess."

He got up and went into the kitchen, came back with a beer and a pack of cigarettes.

"Thanks," I said when he handed me the beer. He nodded

30

and sat down. "I guess Trish told you that I'm staying here a couple days."

"Yeah. I saw you last night, but you were sleeping."

"Sorry to intrude."

Joey shrugged and took a gulp from his beer. He shook out a cigarette from the pack and lit it. "How come you're not staying at your Mom's?"

"She pissed me off. She's a handful. Have you met her?"

"Yeah, once. Mostly I've heard about her from Trish."

"I bet." Joey smiled. "She threw out my pot," I said. He nodded, sympathetic, and sucked on his cigarette. *Law & Order: SVU* was on again. We watched it for a minute while we drank our beers.

"She's hot," Joey said. I looked at him. He motioned to the TV. "That Mariska Hargitay."

"I can't believe you know her name," I said, laughing.

Joey smirked at me, took a drag. "Your sister gets mad when I say girls are hot."

"He's more my speed," I said when they cut to Christopher Meloni.

Joey smiled. "Yeah, he's hot, I guess," he said.

I felt my cock shift. Apparently, Trish had told him about me and he was all right with it.

Joey took another drink of his beer. "I bet he's got a big dick," he said.

"Yeah," I said, then nervously changed the subject. "So, what do you do at work exactly, Joey?"

"We're building this garage out at the Westinghouse factory. Like, for employees. Part underground, part above. I been doing that since last summer."

"Trish said you do woodworking?"

"Yeah," Joey said, reaching to snuff out his cigarette in the ashtray. His shirt rode up his back. I could see the white strip of his lower back just before it disappeared into his shorts, the hint of curvature where his ass began. He sat back. "My dad and I, we got a shop. It's just a garage, really. But we make, like, tables and bookshelves. Sell 'em sometimes. Actually, I haven't been there in a while. But my grandpa did it, too. He taught my dad and my dad taught me."

"That's cool," I said, genuinely impressed. It seemed like the perfect thing, to be born into a trade. Instead of doing what I was doing, flailing about trying to make something out of myself.

Then Trisha opened the bedroom door. She was half-asleep, her hair standing up from her head in a gravity-defying cascade. "Hey," she said and looked at Joey. "What are you doing?"

"Havin' a beer before I come to bed."

"Come to bed," she said.

"Soon as I have this beer," he said. She shut the door. Joey tipped back the beer and gulped the rest of it. He crushed the can in his hand and winked at me. "Duty calls," he said.

I let that pass without comment. "Goodnight," I said, and he nodded as he disappeared into the bedroom.

4

Trish made so much goddamn noise in the morning as she got ready for work. It almost made me regret leaving Mom's. After what felt like hours of lying on the couch, trying to ignore her slamming cupboard doors, clomping around the kitchen floor in her high heels, and turning on the loudest fucking coffee maker I've ever heard, she started vacuuming. I got up and stood in the kitchen door, wiping the crud out of my eyes.

"Jesus Christ, Trish. Do you have to vacuum right now? It's six in the morning."

"I spilled coffee grounds," she said, screwing up her face at me. "It's not my fault you're crashing on my couch."

"If I didn't know better, I'd think you were trying to wake me up."

"I'm just trying to act like you aren't here," she said, sitting and pulling a compact out of her purse and eyeliner.

"Thanks," I said and walked toward the bathroom. She shrugged and looked in the mirror, lined her eyes.

The house was quiet after she left, quieter than quiet. We were deep in the forest, really. Cars rarely went by.

I tried to go back to sleep and I did, for a minute. I woke to sounds coming from the bedroom, but it quickly got quiet. Joey was in there. I was instantly awake, alert. I heard him rustling around on the bed.

I started to imagine him in there and me out here in a house in the middle of the woods while my sister was at work.... I wondered what he wore when he slept. Something told me he slept naked.

My cock shot up, then became throbbingly, pulsatingly hard. The bedroom went quiet, but my fantasies kept raging. I was wearing boxer briefs. I tucked my hand underneath the waistband and felt my cock, tweaked the head of it. Then I licked my fingers and got the head slippery.

The sounds started again: more rustling, then a brief blast of tinny sound that quickly faded. It made me think of a TV, but I realized that it was probably coming from a laptop, maybe from somebody clicking on a video that started louder than they'd expected.

I stroked myself under my boxers, under a blanket. I became convinced that he was jerking off in there, about four yards and one wall away from where I was touching myself.

Finally, I couldn't resist. I got up from the couch and crept across the carpet to the door of their bedroom. I put my ear to it and caught the low sound of porn coming from a crappy laptop speaker. Then a low exhalation from Joey. A moan?

I ran back to the couch, laid down, threw the blanket over myself, and grabbed my cock. Imagined him in that bed, on those silk sheets, toned body writhing, his hand polishing his diamond-hard cock, head of it pink as a pig's snout, and maybe his other hand sliding back toward his pale-pink butt, fingertips darting against his wrinkled hole....

It took me about five seconds to come.

That was all I needed, I told myself as I grabbed my dirty sock from the day before and scooped the come from my bellybutton. *Just the fantasy of it*.

I went into the bathroom and washed my hands. When I came out, he was up and in the kitchen. Washing his hands.

"Morning," he said, his languid, satisfied face shining in the morning sunlight. I nodded and sat back onto the couch. Joey walked toward the bathroom. He was wearing blue pajama pants, and I could see the flop of his cock at the front of them. He shut the door and took a piss. I turned behind me and looked into the bedroom. A black laptop, open, sat on the disheveled bed. There was a box of tissues next to it.

I walked to the porn store that day. It wasn't a long walk, but it was a strange one. I had to go down my sister's hill and through a meadow to get on the train tracks, which eventually ran alongside the highway.

There were a lot of cars in the store's lot. Randy introduced me to the woman who was working the front, a dark-haired woman named Rita.

"She's sticking around for another hour, but then it's just me and you. I hope you're all right with trying it on your own tonight? I mean, I'll be around, but I have to run out to Walmart at some point."

"For what?" I asked.

"Paper towels," he said, laughing. I followed him through the store and into the back booth area, which I hadn't seen the night before. It was dark back there. It smelled like disinfectant and other things. It was basically set up like a maze, with matte-black partitions creating borders around booths so that you couldn't see inside as you passed. "Paper towels were one of the first things I added when I took this place over two years ago. Just a rack in each booth. The previous owners, they didn't want to acknowledge what went on back here. But this helps a lot with cleanup, believe me."

There were men hanging around, leaning against walls and wandering through the booths, their faces glowing red from the lights that were on each individual booth, a light that told you whether the booth was occupied or not. In this context, it seemed that red could either mean stop or go, depending on who was in there.

"Busy night," Randy said, raising his eyebrows at me. We reached a back door with an "Employees Only" placard tacked to it. Randy pushed the pressure bar, and we were in a hallway piled with supplies and old porno promotional materials. A life-sized cutout of a woman who looked like Nick's mom posed with a huge dildo. Randy put a key in the office door and ushered me inside.

"Have a seat," he said and sat at his desk. "Women aren't allowed in the back room, by the way. Some weird state law."

"Is that to keep people from having sex back there?"

"People *are* having sex back here, believe me. But they say no women, so no women it is."

I filled out my W-9.

Randy said, "You can go back there anytime you want, but not on your shift. It's just a bad idea. You gotta watch the store."

"No problem. I really have no intention of going back there."

"Not the type, eh?" Randy said in a warm way. "Everybody's

36

different," he added, which seemed to imply that he *was* the type. I smiled at him, digging his honesty.

"Mostly, you're going to be running the register and trying to sell things to people. About seventy-five percent of our customers are just going into the back. It'll be five-dollar sets of coupons, all night. They have to buy coupons to go into the booths. However, they can leave to go outside and come back, if nature calls. That was also one of my innovations," he said, looking proud. "Before that, we used to have a lot more piss back there."

"But you still do?"

"Yeah," Randy said. "It happens. You'll have to mop it up."

"But nothing worse than that?"

"Nothing worse than that," Randy assured me.

If you ever wonder what type of guy goes into a bookstore, well, it takes all kinds. Even on that first night, I saw white guys, black guys, older, younger. Guys in suits and guys in muddy boots. It would have never occurred to me to get sex in a place like this. I could understand why it would turn people on, though it still didn't do anything for me.

A skinny guy in thick brown glasses with a wrinkled face kept wandering around the entrance before disappearing back into the darkness. He was there for hours.

"That's Lloyd," Randy said, looking up at me from an inventory sheet. "He's always here. He hunts dick like it's... Moby Dick, I suppose. And he's Captain Ahab."

Randy left a few minutes later. I rung up one customer for the back. There were at least fifteen people back there, judging from the cars I could see in the lot, yet there was nobody in the

37

store. A few guys left, looking at me askance. And then Lloyd came up to the counter.

"Hey, guy," he said in a tiny voice. "Somebody took a shit back there."

"What?" I could barely hear him, and maybe I was hoping I wasn't hearing what I thought I heard.

"A dump. In the booth."

I made an executive decision, my very first. Found the light switch for the back, flipped it on, kicked everybody out (even Lloyd). Randy pulled up just as everybody was leaving. He looked at me like I was crazy.

I told him what Lloyd had told me.

"No!" he said in total disbelief.

We ventured into the back together, creeping on the balls of our feet, afraid of what lurked around each corner. Finally, we found it in booth eleven. I won't go into details, but it was, fortunately, a rather contained mess, almost as if somebody had left us a horrible little gift right on the bench.

Of course, we took pictures on our phones.

"You have to clean it up," Randy said, looking at me wildly.

"No!" I screamed.

"Oh my God." He steeled himself. "Okay. I'm gonna do it." He grabbed my arm. "You have to stay with me," he said.

I did, like a good employee. I laughed until I cried, and Randy laughed, too. It was a bonding experience. "I swear to you, I've owned this place for three years, and in that whole time, I've never had that happen. But you conjured it! When you asked if we had to clean up anything worse than that. It's your fault," he said.

I shook my head, laughing still.

◆

Demoralization set in on my walk home that night. I couldn't even let the relief of having a job sit with me for more than twenty-four hours. I wanted to be in New York City making art, or *anywhere* making art, but instead I was cleaning up shit.

Trish was home. Joey wasn't.

"When do you start your new career in pornography?" she asked.

"I started it tonight," I said.

She was in her pajamas. "Randy owns that place, right? Randy Perletti?"

"How do you know him?"

"I don't know. He's one of the only gay guys in town," she said, pouring water into the kettle.

"I think I saw a guy who goes to Mom's church come in."

"If Joey ever goes in there, you have to tell me," she said.

"Why?"

"Cause I wanna know."

"Do *you* think he goes in there?"

"I don't know," she said. She got out a tea bag. "I know he likes porn. He looks at it on my laptop." I laughed, but uneasily, thinking of the morning. "I'm serious. You should see my browser history. Every time I type something in, like, twenty porn sites come up."

"Well, I guess he's smarter than the guys who come into

that store and still actually buy DVDs, not realizing you can get it for free."

"Do people really have sex in that place?"

"Yep. I have to clean come."

"Ew! No!" Trish said, holding her hand out to stop me.

"I cleaned up poop tonight," I said.

"Oh my God!" she said, holding her hand over her mouth.

"I took a picture of it," I said reaching for my cell phone. Then I chased her around the room until she looked at it.

Later, we were watching TV, me on my couch, her on the easy chair. She seemed agitated.

"How many more nights are you staying here?" she asked.

"Actually, Trish. I was thinking...."

"No," she said. "C'mon."

"I can't live with her. She tried to get me to help her out of the shower the other day."

"Why would she do that?" Trisha said, rolling her eyes.

"It's all about her fibromyalgia now. She goes to the doctors, like, five times a week, and she always wants me to drive her. You know how she is. Any opportunity she gets to have us do something for her, she takes it."

Trisha looked at me. She knew. Mom had been like this ever since Dad died. "I'm so grateful to have you, every second of every day," she started saying to us then, which was as rife with responsibility as it was with gratitude. There was a reason Trisha had moved into her own place not long after she'd graduated high school, even if she'd stuck around close to Mom while I'd moved sixty miles away.

"How much are you gonna pay me?"

40

"Rent?" I said.

"Yeah."

"Um...seventy-five a month?"

Trish gave me a "get real" look. "Try two hundred."

"A hundred twenty-five. I do work at a porno store, remember?"

"All right. A hundred twenty-five. But you have to pay your share for the utilities and buy your own groceries."

"Okay. Deal," I said, marveling at how easily I'd given in. One twenty-five was most certainly more than I would've had to start paying Mom if I'd stayed there, but the benefits of living with Trisha more than made up for that.

I had to admit that living with Joey was one of those benefits.

"Will you have to ask Joey first?" I said.

"He won't care. He's used to living with a bunch of people."

"Where'd he move from?"

"This dumpy converted garage off the highway with two other guys. Total bachelor pad. Really *disgusting*," she said, like she relished the word. "That's where this couch came from, actually," she said.

Just then, she got a phone call and took it into the bedroom. I could hear it was a heated conversation, and she looked pissed when she came out.

"What was that?" I said.

"None of your business." She went into the kitchen, bent down, and rifled in a cupboard. When she came back into the living room, she had a beat-up package of menthol cigarettes in her hand and was shaking one out. "Shut up if you know

41

what's good for you," she said, lighting up and taking a drag.

"I'm gonna smoke some pot if you're doing that," I said, taking out the joint I'd planned to smoke in the backyard after she went to bed.

Trisha watched me. "Give me a hit of that," she said.

"I thought you got drug tested?"

"Whatever. They're not gonna test me. I need it anyway, and I can't smoke this fucking cigarette. This pack is, like, six months old."

I exhaled my hit and handed her the lit joint. "So, where's Joey?"

"Hanging out with his friends," she said.

"The guys he used to live with?"

"Yeah. They're having a party." She twirled her finger in the air.

"Do you wish you were invited?"

"No," she said, reaching for the joint again and taking a bigger hit this time. "But I know he's getting trashed, so he'll probably end up passing out there."

"So, that's why you're upset?"

"I'm not upset!" She turned to the TV and we watched in silence while I finished the joint. It wasn't the first time I smoked with her, but it had been a while. "Anyway," she said, "he'll be home eventually. I'm gonna go lay in bed and, I don't know…." Her gaze drifted off in a stoned, distracted way. I laughed at her. "I'm high," she said.

"That's the idea."

She got up. "Hey Nate," she said from the door of her bedroom. I looked back at her. "I'm glad you're home."

42

"Thanks," I said.

I took a shower, but I couldn't fall asleep, so I put on my headphones and listened to music. My iPod fell through the couch cushions and I had to dig for it, and when I did, I felt something, so I pulled it out. It was a pair of men's underwear. Black Calvin Klein briefs, cut pretty high, almost like bikini briefs. Were they Joey's? I remembered Trisha saying that the couch had come from his bachelor pad, but somehow they seemed like the type of underwear that Joey would wear.

It made me horny. I smelled them. There was the faintest hint of masculinity on them. Ball sweat? Ass sweat? Who cared. I ducked my head under the covers, draped them over my face, and had my way with myself.

5

I woke up to Trisha rattling around in the kitchen again. Her hair was pulled back in a severe bun. She seemed even more peeved—Joey had never come home. She asked me to clean off the patio while she was at work. Her heels clacked aggressively on the tile floor of the kitchen as she walked out the door.

I fell back asleep. I was dreaming of something until I realized I was hearing the clink of somebody's keys as they opened the front door. Joey was home.

I had a morning boner, but it was covered with my blanket. I pretended to sleep as he walked quietly into the house. I heard him pissing in the bathroom. I sat up and rubbed my eyes as he came into the living room.

"Hey," he said, smiling his trademark half-grin that made him look simultaneously innocent and devious. He wore a blue T-shirt with "Bohnam's Construction" and a picture of a hammer and pick axe on the front. The sleeves were cut off so you could see his toned arms. His jeans were worn white along his thighs.

"Good morning. Or afternoon."

"I ain't keeping track," he said. He looked at the ceiling, held the bridge of his nose. "I think I'm still drunk," he said.

"Good party?" I said.

Joey shrugged. "Same old, same old, really," he said, crashing onto the easy chair. "Your sister pissed?"

"Yeah."

Joey reached inside his jeans pocket and pulled out a pack of cigarettes. "I coulda come home last night, but at some point, you have to cut your losses. Coming home to your sister when she's pissed at me is never a good thing."

"So, you waited until she left for work. Smart."

Joey winked at me as he lit his cigarette. "Well, plus I just woke up. You working today?"

"Yeah."

"How's the porn store? Trish told me."

"Dirty," I said.

He smiled. "You get a discount?"

"Yeah. Thirty percent."

Joey raised his eyebrows. "Good to know."

I peed, then put a Toaster Strudel in the toaster. When Joey saw it, he asked for one, too. So we sat and watched a cooking show and ate our breakfast.

"I talked with Trisha last night, and I'm basically going to be living here now," I said.

Joey nodded. "That's cool. You could even clean out that attic room, if you want."

"There's an attic in this house?" I said.

"Yep," he said. "C'mon. I'll show you."

I followed him into the bedroom. A piece of art had been added to the wall. It was—I shit you not—a black velvet painting of an entwined couple, all in silhouette: he on top, she on bottom. It was just modern enough to not be completely tasteless, but still: sexy times. "Your sister bought that for me," Joey said when he saw me looking.

"Nice," I said.

45

He went to a small half-door next to the dresser, which I'd assumed was a second closet, but it opened onto a staircase. I followed Joey upstairs.

"It's pretty insane up there right now with the old owner's stuff," he said. "Trisha won't go up here. She wanted me to put the dresser up against the door cause it freaks her out, but I wouldn't." There weren't a lot of steps. We got to the top and were on a wooden floor in the attic. "I'm thinking about making it my den, but maybe it could be your bedroom."

It was surprisingly large, with a window on the far wall that faced the road. Piled in front of it were boxes upon boxes, stacks of framed art, and these weird gigantic stuffed animals—pink and brown-orange monkeys and a giraffe. It was a totally useable room, and it seemed strange to me that Trisha had never mentioned it.

I could smell Joey standing next to me. Stale liquor and cigarettes, but a deeper smell underneath, a musky guy odor. "I don't know," I said. "It might be weird to have to go through the bedroom to get up here."

"That's a good point," Joey said. Being so close to him, I could really see how undeniably attractive he was, his blue eyes sparkling even in the dim light of the attic. He raised an eyebrow at me. "Might see something you shouldn't."

"Right," I said. There was a loaded moment where we both just stood there. Was he imagining me catching him having sex with my sister? I got the feeling that we were both turned on, that if I were to reach out and feel his cock (which was only about a foot away from my hand) it would be hard and he would want me to touch it, get down on my knees, and take

46

it in my mouth.

A floorboard creaked under my foot and it broke the spell.

"I need a shower," Joey said. I followed him down the steps into the bedroom and shut the attic door behind us.

I figured I should get dressed and looked at my pile of clothes, the combined spillage from my two travel bags. Really, living out of a living room is less than ideal. Joey came out of the bedroom with some folded clothes—on top was a wifebeater—and took them into the bathroom. It didn't sound like he locked the door, not that I had any intention of going in there.

I got dressed, allowing myself one minute of standing there naked in the living room and imagining him naked in the shower just a few feet away. I was on the couch, reading my book when he came out, wearing the wifebeater and a pair of track pants. I wondered if he was wearing underwear underneath them and if they looked anything like the briefs I had found earlier that morning.

When I brushed my teeth, I saw his dirty clothes in a pile on the floor and resisted the urge to dig through them.

When I came out, Joey was holding a packed glass pipe. "I was going to smoke this before I go back to bed. Wanna join me?"

We sat on the back deck, which was next to the little backyard. It was a serene morning. The sun illuminated a patch of bright green grass, and birds fluttered in the trees.

We talked about his car, about his wood shop. "I'm making a bookshelf for your sister cause she likes to read so much," he said, which I thought was sweet. "Trisha said you make art?"

"Yeah. I went to school for anthropology, but I've always

been into drawing."

"She said you won an award?"

"Aw, just some stupid thing in high school," I said, feeling my defenses go up. It was always like this when I wound up talking about me and my art. As much as I wanted to make something of myself, I felt suspicious of those impulses.

"Still, that's cool. And your dad was a writer, right?"

"Yeah. Well, he only wrote one book."

"That's cool," Joey said. He was smoking a cigarette, and now he snubbed it out. "Welp, I'm going to bed."

I bid him good night. I cleaned off the back deck like my sister asked me to. I peeked into the bedroom window, but the blinds were drawn.

Mom kept calling to remind me that she needed me to take her to the post office. I started ignoring her after the third reminder, but I still walked to her house and drove her into town.

"They said I have a package, but I don't understand this thing," she said, handing me a pink slip of paper.

"It says you have a package," I said, putting the car in park. I waited with her in line. She wound up getting a big box from a home shopping network.

"What is it?" I asked.

"I can't remember."

"Seriously?"

Mom shrugged and dug into her purse. She pulled out a small brass key. "Let's see if your father got any mail," she said, the key pointing her way as she rounded the corner of the post office to the wall-sized grid of metal boxes. I knew that she'd maintained a post-office box for Dad, the one where he received fan mail since his book was published, but I'd never actually gone with her to see it. The numbers "428" were embossed into the gray metal door. Mom inserted the key, opened the door, and brought out two letters.

I ducked down and look through the box, caught a brief view of the post office through the open back of the box: blue pants walking around, carts, and a dirty linoleum floor. Mom swung the box shut and locked it.

"Why do they write fan mail to a dead person? It makes no fucking sense," I said.

"Watch your mouth," Mom said. She dropped the key back into her purse. "They're lonely people, I think. It's really been only the same two lately, though I wonder how much time they have left. Carol is seventy-six, I think? And Henry got rectal cancer...well, I think that's been two years now, so maybe he's doing better."

"That's nice that you know who they are."

"An unread letter is a terrible thing. I can't let that happen, even if this blasted box costs me ten dollars a month. Sometimes I feel like I should ask Carol and Henry for it," she said. I laughed.

Dad had never made a ton of money off his book, but it had gone back into print a few times over the years, once more recently, so Mom occasionally got royalty checks to supplement what she got in Social Security. She never had a job that I could remember. When she met my dad, they were both living in

49

Pittsburgh, and his book had just been published. For some reason, they moved to Groom, which was Dad's hometown, and he married Mom here. Dad went to work for the *Groom Gazette*, the local newspaper, as an editor. They didn't have us until they were older; Mom was in her late thirties when she had Trisha.

"Do you ever write them back?" I asked.

"No."

"Do they know who you are?"

"No, but they know their letters don't get returned."

She opened the package once we got back to the house. "It's a foot bath," she said with a sense of wonder.

"Oh," I said. "Why do you need that?"

"It's for relaxation. It promotes foot health."

"You buy a lot of that crap, don't you?" I said, looking around her kitchen at the electric quesadilla maker and the microwave egg cooker.

"Not very much," she said, but it seemed to me that the stuff-to-space ratio in our house had increased incrementally each year since Dad died.

When I'd finished eating the grilled cheese sandwich Mom made me, I figured it was now or never. "I got a job," I said. The way her face lit up just about killed me.

"You did?"

"At the adult store on the highway," I said, and that light got snuffed out real quick.

"Oh, for heaven's sake," she said. "You didn't."

"I did. It's just a job. They're paying me."

"To do what?"

"To prostitute myself. No!" I quickly said because she looked like she actually believed me. "Mom, I'm just working the register. It's just a store like any other store." *Except men fuck each other and shit in it,* I thought, but didn't say.

Mom shook her head. "I guess I shouldn't be surprised," she said.

"What is that supposed to mean?"

"I mean the way you kids are. Your sister is dating that Joey, and I'm *sure* he's spending the night at her house. Isn't he?"

"What does that have to do with me working at the porn store?" I said. It bothered me the way it was tied up in Mom's mind and how Trisha's transgression was worse than mine, which was somehow expected.

"It's disgusting. I don't want to hear anything about it," she said.

I went to the sink and washed my plate.

She asked, "Have you ever seen Dan Granger in there?"

"Dan Granger? No, why?"

"Well, he got arrested last year in the park."

"Promised Land?" Promised Land State Park was on the edge of Groom and was a known gay cruising spot. I'd gone to high school with Dan Granger and had never had any indication he was gay, so that was interesting.

"Yes. Lewdness."

"He used to spit on people in seventh grade," I said.

"Well, there you go."

6.

I worked until the evening, my first shift on my own, and it was great, mainly because I didn't have to go into the back at all.

When I got to Trisha's, Joey was cooking in an apron. "I'm making meatballs," he said. Trisha was still in her business suit. I sat down at the table.

"Did you know Mom still has Dad's P.O. box? And that he still gets letters?"

"I think I knew that. I don't understand why people liked that book. I thought it was skeezy."

"Skeezy?" Joey said, looking up from the counter.

"Yeah, there's all this sex...I mean, it's not explicit, but some of it is a little...less than sexy. Especially since my Dad wrote it."

"She's talking about the transgender Martians."

"Yeah, some of the males have vaginas and the females have penises. It's so weird. It totally freaked me out when I read it in junior high."

"That's the reason why that book has stayed in print," I said. Some people took it up as a transgender text, even if it wasn't explicitly so.

"So, Trish," Joey said, "I was talking to Nate this morning, and we were thinking, since he's gonna be staying here, maybe we could clean out the attic and he could stay up there."

"The attic?" Trisha said, almost like she didn't know what we were talking about. "Really?"

"I mean, we're not using it for anything," Joey said.

Trisha picked up a carrot stick and took a bite. I grabbed one for myself. Honestly, I didn't know how I felt about staying up there, and it seemed strange to me that Joey was so into the idea.

"I don't know," Trisha said finally, shooting me a quick glance and looking away. "I mean, I'd love for you guys to clean it out. Joey, you can move all your stuff up there from the basement."

"Yeah," I said, trying to save the awkwardness. "I'll just crash on the couch."

"I mean, maybe you can sleep up there sometimes. It's just that, you'd have to go through the bedroom...."

"I know."

We both looked at Joey, who just kept rolling his meatballs.

"You guys want to play a game tonight?" I said, trying to change the subject.

"We're going to see a movie," Trisha said. "Right, babe?"

Joey nodded.

I got this weird pang. It took me a moment to realize it was jealousy.

I woke up that morning (for the second time, after Trisha had left and I fell back asleep) and lay on the couch, listening intently to every creak in the house to try and make out if Joey would jack off again. My mind was coursing with fantasies. I wound up jacking off twice, but I never heard anything from his room.

Finally, he came out in just a pair of boxer shorts. I was in my boxer shorts, too. It was a hot morning. He gave the slightest glance over at my body as he passed the couch. I was awake, reading my book. I nodded at him in what I hoped was a non-anxious way.

"Morning," he said. He poured cereal into a bowl. "Want some breakfast?"

"Sure," I said.

He grabbed another bowl off the shelf and poured cereal into it. "Breakfast," he said, smiling at me.

I sat down, and he poured milk into my bowl. We looked at each other over our bowls, crunching.

Joey said, "We should get stoned today."

And so we did. We went into the backyard, on the deck, the sunlight beaming down. "So fucking hot in that bedroom," Joey said, running his hand over his stomach. "That's why I had to strip down."

I sat on the lounge chair and rolled a joint, half with his stuff, half with mine, then lit it up.

"How old are you?" he asked me.

"Twenty-one."

"I'm twenty-two."

"Oh, wow. I thought you were older." Trisha was twenty-four. Joey shrugged.

"Should we clean out the attic today?" I suggested. Just saying it got me turned on, to think of being alone with Joey up there.

"Yeah, we could start that. I'm still hungry, though."

Joey thought it was too much work to make food at the house, so we ordered a pizza and drove to pick it up. It was the first time I'd been in his car. We put shorts on, but didn't bother putting on shirts.

It was the first time I'd been in his car, and I was high on a beautifully hot summer day. It had a tape deck and a few tapes lying around on the floor. "From the guy who sold it to me," Joey said. One of them was Neil Young, so I put that on and it sounded just perfect.

The back seat was wide and deep. I had this fantasy of a man driving me off the road into a field and then into a glen where he would fuck me under a waterfall.

But that didn't happen. We drove into town, past Trisha's bank. I wondered what she would think if she saw us, if she would think it strange. But it wasn't. Just two roommates, friends, whatever, driving around.

It was after we got home and ate the pizza that it happened. I lay on the couch in the combination food coma/weed hangover. He was kicked back on the easy chair.

"I'm gonna take a nap," he said. The chair creaked as he got up. "Gonna take a shower first."

"Why?" I said, half asleep.

"I like to sleep clean," he said.

He walked around the couch and went into the bedroom, but he didn't close the door. I could see right into the room from where I was lying, but he never looked at me looking at him. He went to the dresser, opened a drawer, and took out a pair of underwear. He turned away from me and slid off his shorts, standing there naked, his hot ass on full display,

55

fiddling around with the briefs in his hands before stepping into them. Then he walked back into the living room.

I showered blessings on whatever gods gave me that particular bit of fantasy material for later use, though I suspected it had less to do with deities and more to do with Joey himself. He didn't act like he was showing off, but he was showing off—or maybe he didn't care either way.

He came out of the bathroom a half hour later, wearing the fresh briefs and drying his hair with a towel. He stood over me, still lying on the couch, now reading my book, his packed crotch in my face, skin still glistening wet from the shower.

"Night, night," he said.

◆

I fell asleep, too. I woke up to Trisha walking in the door.

"Jesus, are you just waking up?" she said. I looked at my phone: It was six o'clock. Luckily, I didn't have to work that night. I sat up. Trisha was wearing her office clothes, and she looked like the day had used her up. She must have worn her hair swept up in the morning, but now it looked like a fallen cake. "What did you do today?"

"Um...smoked some pot?"

She looked at me lying on the couch, looking for all the world like the bum she thought I was. "I thought maybe you guys would start on the attic."

"We never got around to it."

She sneered—actually *sneered* at me—and went into the bedroom.

56

I sulked. I was pissed at her for being pissed at me, but there was more to it than that. When I heard sounds coming from the bedroom that sounded like sex sounds, movements and grunts that could have been something else, but surely weren't, I got even more annoyed.

I got dressed and left the house, walked down the road and smoked more pot. Everything seemed like shit. I was stuck in a house with my sister and her boyfriend. I hadn't drawn a fucking line since I got back from college (actually, I hadn't drawn all that much my last year of college either), and I was harboring this ridiculous dream of moving to New York City and...what? Being discovered? Living on the street? Getting a job at a *different* porn store?

I was stuck in Groom with a fucking college degree. I'd had such a feeling of superiority over my sister and my mother when I was in college. I was doing what neither of them had had the courage or energy to do. It had given me something to go on, an aura of respect, which was something I'd never experienced before. But now it was over and what the fuck did I have? A job at a porn store and pretensions of being an artist.

The next day I had to work, but I was determined to make something of myself before I went in. I figured I'd start cleaning up the attic, but Joey was asleep for most of the morning and I didn't want to creep through the bedroom.

When Joey finally did wake up, he came out in his pajama pants and sat across from me. I told him my ambition for the day.

"It's gonna be hot up there," he said. It already was a hot day, and you could tell it was going to be a real scorcher.

"I know, but it's now or never."

"You wanna get high first?"

I acted like I had to think about it. "Sure," I said. "Backyard?"

"Too hot," Joey said. "Let's go in the bedroom."

And so we did. Joey shut the door behind us, and I got this fluttery feeling in my stomach that wasn't just the anticipation of getting stoned. There was a smell in that bedroom that was more than just the smell of the scented candles that my sister had clustered all around the dressers and on the bed stand. It was sex, maybe, or just the musky smell of a guy. Joey.

He sat on the bed, so I sat beside him. The covers were all bunched up. The fact that it felt weird was mitigated by the fact that it was cool in there, being that it was at the back of the house and shaded by the hillside that rose above.

Joey packed up his glass pipe, took a hit, and passed it to me.

"So, are you gonna use the attic or just clean it out?" he asked.

"I'm just gonna clean it out for you guys, make myself useful, since I'm not paying all that much in rent."

"That's cool. I guess it would be weird for you to be sleeping up there."

"Yeah," I said.

"I'll help you. I'm gonna make a room out of it, put all my stuff up there from my old place. I've got, like, a hookah and a stereo and all kinds of stuff." He took another hit. "I'm glad you're staying here, though."

"Yeah?"

"Yeah. I like having you around." When we'd finished the

58

bowl and were thoroughly stoned, Joey stood up and went to the dresser. He put his pipe back into the little wooden box he'd taken it out of earlier, then put it into the bottom drawer. I watched him hesitate for a second, then he opened up the top drawer.

"Hey Nate," he said. "Look at this." I looked over at him. He pulled a pink dildo out of the drawer.

"Gross," I said, and my body tensed. I mean, it *was* kind of gross because I figured it was Trisha's. But the fact that he was showing it to me....

Joey laughed. "Don't act like you've never seen one before," he said.

"I see them every day. I *sell* them every day. But that's my sister's."

"Who said it's hers?" he said, laughing. He twisted the knob on the bottom until I could hear it softly buzzing.

"Oh, what. Is it yours?"

"It's for both of us," he said, holding it there for a minute. Then he shut it off and slipped it back into the drawer. "Sorry," he said.

"It's okay," I said. I was almost sick with the anxiety of it, the attraction I felt to him, the way he flirted with me, his unabashed sexuality. "You guys like to get a little freaky, I guess?"

"Gotta keep things interesting," Joey said. "I'm definitely a little freaky." The way he said it, I started getting turned on. And I thought I noticed some extra mass, some solidity in the front of his pajama pants as he reached for the attic door and opened it. He looked at me looking at him and smirked. "Well, let's get to work, I guess," he said.

It was like a sauna up there. We got a fan from downstairs and put it in the window. Then we piled up all the old stuff against one wall. We found a sofa bed that was in good shape. Even the mattress was pretty intact.

In fact, once we got going on it, we had it pretty much cleared. We moved all the old stuff from up there down into the basement with the thought of having it picked up by St. Vincent de Paul. Most of it was junk, though.

We moved Joey's stuff upstairs and set up his "opium den," which was his hookah and a bunch of big pillows that we sat on a rolled-up rug that we'd found. All in all, the place ended up looking pretty great. We had to break in the smoking area, so Joey packed up the pipe.

"Joey, what do your parents do?" I said.

"My mom's a nurse. My dad doesn't do anything."

"Doesn't he do the woodworking with you?"

Joey shook his head. "Hardly ever. He just gets drunk all the time."

"You both have a shop, though, right?"

"Yeah. He worked construction, too, like me. But he doesn't do any of that anymore. I wanna read your Dad's book," he added.

"There's at least one copy at Mom's. Trisha hates that book."

"Why?"

"It's full of seduction. Not sex, exactly, but all this...erotic intrigue, I guess you could call it. Not to mention the gender stuff."

"So, why doesn't she like it? If it's about sex."

"I don't know," I said, treading carefully. "I guess Trisha always seemed weirded out about sex when we were growing up. Maybe she's not like that anymore."

Joey knocked some cobwebs out of the corner. "Man, I love sex," he said.

I laughed. "Me, too. Especially since I'm not getting any of it lately."

"Yeah?"

"Not much going on in this town by way of homos. Certainly not any gay bars."

"Not the porno store?" Joey said.

"Not my scene."

Joey said, "We should drive up to the city some weekend and hit up a gay bar. Get you laid," and I nodded. "We'll take Trisha."

"She'll never do that," I said.

Trisha wasn't homophobic by any means, but we'd never really discussed my sexuality in any detail. Maybe that was just something you didn't talk about with a sibling, but I'd often wished I could talk about boys with her, especially when I was having boyfriend troubles in college. The whole thing with Nick complicated matters. She liked to jab me about it, and I assumed she understood that Nick had meant something to me before they'd dated, but I never told her exactly what had gone down.

"That's cool that you're not homophobic," I said.

"I'm not," Joey said. "My dad, he is."

We worked quietly. I thought of my dad. I didn't come out

until after he died. I'd never felt particularly close to him. I always wondered if that would've changed. When he died, I was thirteen and I mostly hated him. He was quiet and distant. He would come home from work and go into his study in the basement, read and write and do whatever it was that he did in there. The study was strictly forbidden to all of us, even my mom.

He died at work at the newspaper, at his desk. A massive stroke. We never even knew he had high blood pressure, but that was that—he left for work one day and came home in a coffin.

They got me out of class and told me and Trisha. I remember feeling like I didn't know how I should act. They sent us home, so Trisha and I played Monopoly in her room. I remember having fun and trying to be quiet so Mom wouldn't hear.

Then one night, I woke up crying. And Trisha heard me and came into bed with me and we held each other and cried. Which was weird because we'd never been physically close like that, but it felt good, and we held onto each other tightly.

It was after that when Trisha started, like, parenting me. And my mom just checked out. I never saw Trisha cry after that night, about Dad or about anything.

"Do you have any siblings?" I said.

"No. Only child. I've lived with girls before, though. My first girlfriend, I moved in with her while I was still in high school."

We stretched out on the rug. I started to drift off, but when I opened my eyes, Joey was looking at me.

"Hey Nate," he said.

"Yeah?"

"Do you think I'm hot?"

"No," I lied.

"C'mon. You wouldn't go for it?"

I was speechless. But just then, we heard a car coming up the driveway. Trisha…. I was simultaneously annoyed and relieved.

"Hello?" Trish said from downstairs.

"Up here," Joey said and glanced at me before he grabbed a cigarette from the pack and lit it. "Won't she be surprised," he said, meaning the attic.

I collected my breath. I tried to look like I was innocent, but wasn't I?

"Where are you?" she said as she trudged up the attic steps. She looked tired. "I could smell pot from the driveway," she said.

"So what?" I said.

"So nothing," she said. "Whoa," she said, looking around the attic. "Hey," she said to Joey, who stood up and kissed her. She wrapped her arms around his waist, her fingertips flirting with the top of his butt. "I can't believe you managed to clean this out as much as you did. Save some space for me. I might want to make this into my sewing room," she said.

"When was the last time you sewed anything?" I said, hating how nasty I sounded.

Trisha turned to me: weary, over it. "Cause I haven't had the space for it," she said. She turned to Joey. "I'm glad you've got your little man den, or whatever."

Joey led her downstairs by the hand. I waited a bit before I came down after them.

7

Dinner at Mom's. Joey didn't come.

"So, how are the living arrangements?" Mom asked, setting down a humungous bowl of coleslaw that I knew we were going to have to take back to Trish's and pretend to eat and love.

Trisha forked green beans into her mouth, chewed. "Fine," she said. I admired her ability to act innocent in the glare of Mom's interrogations, which were just gearing up.

"And your boyfriend?"

I looked at Mom, looked at Trisha. It was like a tennis match of passive-aggression.

"*Joey* is fine," she said and kept eating.

"We cleaned out the attic," I said.

Trisha let her fork drop, just slightly, as she glared at me.

"You and Joey?" Mom said.

"Yeah. You know, he comes by a lot."

"He lives there, actually," Trisha said, looking Mom straight in the eye. Mom's face tensed up. "That's what you're fishing for, right? Yes, we're living together. Living in sin."

"I knew it," she said, standing and picking up her plate. "I knew it all along," she said as she tossed what was left of her food into the trash.

"Well, I didn't tell you because I knew you'd make a big godda...a big deal out of it."

Mom, never looking at Trisha, took her plate to the sink and turned on the water. I guess dinner was over. "Well, it's one way to get a man," she said. "So much for the peace of living alone, right? Isn't that what you told me when you moved out of here?"

"I think I said something about being an *adult*, too, Mom. Remember that? The fact that I'm twenty-four years old, for the love of Christ."

"Don't take the Lord's name in vain!" Mom said.

"This is fascinating, but I'm going to take a walk," I said, removing myself from the table, glad to be ignored for once. Before I got out the door, I caught something about Mom being abandoned just so Trisha could live as a hedonist.

I walked back to Trisha's. There was an unfamiliar car in the driveway. Trisha pulled up just as I got there. When she saw the car, her face fell.

"Oh, that's just what I need. Bev's here," she said, plastic container of coleslaw in hand.

Sure enough, Joey and a big dumb-looking guy were taking up residence on the sofa. A thick cloud of marijuana smoke hovered over them.

"Hey babe," Joey said, as sweet as could be, hopping up to give her a kiss. Trisha let him kiss her on the cheek, but never took her eyes from the bachelor-pad scene before her. Several empty beer cans sat on the coffee table. One was being used as an ashtray, another had tipped and poured a sticky puddle that someone had tried to mop up with junk mail.

I sat on the easy chair and introduced myself to Joey's friend Bev, who gave me a lazy smile and handed me the joint they were passing.

"Hey Trisha," Bev said. He lifted the can of beer that was nestled in his crotch and took a drink. Burped.

"Hello, Beverly," Trisha said. She went into the bedroom and closed the door. A minute later, she peeked out.

"Joey, come here for a minute," she said, furiously brushing her long red hair. She'd stripped off her shirt and was wearing a tank top. Joey exchanged a glance with Bev and went into the bedroom. I listened to their voices—well, mostly hers—raised and angry. Bev took a hit off the joint and handed it back to me.

"Love," he said, raising his eyebrows and taking a gulp of his beer. By the time Joey came back, the joint was done and Bev was crushing the can. Bev got the message and got up to leave, and soon as he did, Trisha was all over the house, spraying it with air freshener. I migrated to the kitchen and poured a bowl of cereal.

"Your sister doesn't like my friends, Nate," Joey said to me.

"That's not true," Trisha said. "It's just *that one*."

"Why?" Joey said, lighting a cigarette. Trisha glared at it. Joey sat back, seemingly amused by it all.

Trisha set the can of air freshener on the counter where it clinked solidly. She turned to Joey. "He's a sloth. He doesn't do shit."

"He works at the gas station," he said.

Trisha rolled her eyes.

"What's wrong with working at the gas station?" I said.

"Nothing," Trisha said. "But it's, like, he doesn't have a

plan. I mean, Joey, you've got the wood shop."

"I'm never gonna make money off that," Joey said.

"I can't talk about this right now," Trisha said and glared at me like *I'd* started it. "I'm going to bed." She shut the door.

"Guess I should go do damage control," Joey said, snubbing out his cigarette.

"Guess so."

"She just needs to get laid, you know."

My heart quickened. This was the oldest cliché in the book—misogynist, and about my sister, no less—but him saying it to me, in that moment, was something else.

Joey said, "That's what it is with a lot of girls. They get worked up, and you have to fuck it out of them. Maybe all people are like that, though." He rested his arms on his head, making his biceps bulge and revealing the sweaty brush of his armpit hair. "Don't you feel better after you, you know, come?"

"Yeah," I said.

"It's different for guys, though. Like, it doesn't matter who I get it from. Girls, they have to care about you first or something." He looked at me. "Have you ever had sex with a girl?"

"Nope."

"You know what girls are like, though."

"Yeah. Sure."

"It's different. Like, I just want to get my dick wet. You know?"

My heart was really racing now. It felt like he was hitting on me, but I either couldn't believe it or didn't want to believe it.

I nodded. Joey got up and went to bed. I did the same.

68

I worked the next night. I felt as horny as I ever had in my whole life. Sometimes I think I used this horniness as an excuse for what happened with Joey the next night, what set it all off.

Randy came out of the office about an hour into my shift. I looked up from the *Playboy* I'd been reading—for the articles, of course.

"I can't be back there anymore," he said, rubbing his eyes. "I need to hire somebody to do this inventory shit. I hate it." He leaned against the counter and looked at my *Playboy*. "Anything good in that?"

"No. I'm trying to take my mind off things. I'm so horny that I think I'm gonna go crazy."

"That right?" Randy said, giving me a look. I'd be lying if I didn't think about it. Older guys had never been my thing, though I knew some gay guys got into that. Still, Randy wasn't a bad-looking guy for his age, with his dark-but-graying Italian features and strong body. "Maybe your standards are too high?"

"You're definitely right about that. I've really only had sex with two people," I said.

"You're kidding me."

"Nope. Just my friend Nick in high school and my boyfriend in college. Oh, wait...."

"Yeah, I figured," he said.

I laughed. "There were a couple other guys at college," I said. "One-night-stand sort of things."

"Wow. I don't know if I admire your piety or pity it,"

Randy said.

I shrugged. "Just the way I'm wired," I said. There was something disembodied about the back-room sex that turned me off. The casual sex I'd had in college had been drunk and desperate. I liked being with people who were close to me. Eric, my college boyfriend, had started out as my best friend, just like Nick had in high school. Eric had been openly queer, thankfully.

Nick didn't seem to be an option anymore. I was jerking off a lot, mostly while I was taking a shower cause that seemed more respectful. I never heard Joey doing it again.

Randy said, "Yeah, well, don't short-circuit yourself. Everybody needs sex. And it's all around you."

I thought, *Maybe that's the problem*. Because while nothing about the porn store antics in the back room turned me on, there were guys who I found attractive. Plus, there was gay porn all around the store. I was dying to watch some on my laptop, but I didn't really have the space for it at my sister's.

"Truth be told, this store is the most sex I see these days, but they used to show up at my back door. Literally," he said.

"Yeah?"

"Yeah. One of the benefits of being openly gay in a small town. Everyone knew who we were."

"Do you have a partner?"

"I did. He died about two years ago."

"Oh, I'm sorry."

Randy waved his hand, but I could tell that it was still close for him, emotionally. We got harassed a lot, too," he said. "We'd get egged to hell on Halloween. Once we got spray painted. It's died down recently, maybe cause the gays are so acceptable now. Who knows? It's probably just cause I'm old hat. People don't notice me anymore."

"Aw, c'mon."

He paused. "No, you're right. I'm still hot," he said.

I laughed.

"You really can find some diamonds in the rough back there, though," Randy said. "You know, the 'straight' ones."

I was about to tell Randy how my sister's boyfriend seemed to be flirting with me at every opportunity, and how my fantasy life was dominated by thoughts of doing just about anything and everything with him, when we heard the bell on the door.

"Speak of the devil," Randy said.

A guy walked up to the counter. He never looked at Randy. He barely looked at me. "Five," he said in a flat, almost annoyed voice. He was a real piece, though—the hot suburban dad of somebody's dreams, built like concrete had been poured into his clothes.

"See you in a few minutes," Randy said to me and followed the guy into the back room.

I focused on my *Playboy*. Ten minutes later, the big guy came out, hurried to the door, and left, never once looking at me. Randy followed, a big smile on his face.

"*That one*," he said, shaking his head. "Always good to the last drop."

8

I've tried to remember if I jacked off when I got home that night, as if that would excuse what happened, as if I could absolve myself.

I know I couldn't sleep. I tossed and turned for an hour, two hours—it was hard to tell—then I turned on the TV with the volume real low.

The bedroom door opened quietly. I looked behind me. There was Joey, softly shutting the door. In just his underwear.

They were the briefest of grey briefs, leaving next to nothing to the imagination. He walked over to the easy chair. I watched his hairy thighs flex as he walked, the muscular round dome of his butt that stretched out the high-cut back of his underwear.

"I can't sleep," he said and flopped down in the chair. He spread his legs, draping one over the arm of the chair. Even in the dim, shifting light of the TV, I could see his cock in the pouch, the ridge of the head outlined on the fabric, the two orbs of his nuts.

"Me either," I said.

Joey looked at me, smiled his half-smile. He had one arm resting on the back of the chair. His other hand was on the side of his face, his eyes half closed like he'd been just barely on the surface of sleep.

He looked me in the eyes as he ran his hand across his smooth, white chest, over his pert pink nipples. Then down his tight abs, the treasure trail that went into his briefs. "Your sister's asleep," he said as his hand brushed across his crotch, fluffed it a bit, then came to rest on the inside of his thigh. "I'm too horny to sleep."

I looked at the TV. Turned back to Joey.

"I tried to wake her up, but she wasn't having it," he said.

"Is she still pissed at you?"

"I guess so," Joey said. He kept his hand on his crotch, his face turned to the TV where Elliot Stabler was reaming out a child molester.

My cock was dripping. I sat up a bit, stretched one of my arms over the back of the couch, kept my eyes on the TV. Out of the corner of my eye, I saw Joey watching me. I liked that. If my summer in Groom wasn't treating me well in many respects, it was making me look good. All that walking had made me drop the few pounds I'd gained in college. I had a tan. My chest was thin but broad in the shoulders, my stomach flat and smooth.

I had a blanket over my lap. I tossed it off. I adjusted my shorts, pulling them down just slightly. I have almost no hair on my body. In the dim light of the TV, my stomach looked smooth all the way into my shorts. I looked up. Joey was looking at me.

I was letting him look at me, take in my body. I liked it. It made my cock swell.

My eyes caught his. "What should we do?" he said.

I looked at him, my heart racing. I wasn't going to say it.

He asked, "Want to have a beer?"

"Yeah," I said and let the air out of my lungs.

Joey got up. "I can't remember what we've got," he said. It seemed like I should follow him, so I stood. My cock was tumescent, tenting out the front of my shorts just slightly.

He opened the fridge, bent down to look in, the light of it casting shadows on his pale musculature. His cock seemed to be chubbed up, too. "Bev left some Yuenglings," he said and handed me a bottle.

He leaned against the counter and crossed his legs in front of him. We cracked open our beers. He took a drink and I did the same.

My cock was still plump. His was, too. I looked in his eyes and somehow knew we were both thinking the same thing.

"Should we do something?" he said. His hand went to his crotch, cupping it casually, like it could be mistaken for an unconscious action.

"Like what?" I said, but his cock was getting harder and so was mine, and there was no mistaking anymore what this was. We were right on the precipice, the point of no return. We couldn't laugh it off and pretend like we were talking about something else. This was it.

Joey was a few feet away from me. He rose from the counter, set his beer on it, and took a step toward me. I still had my beer in my hand. I took another gulp and set it on the table.

"Like what I was saying yesterday," he said, his hand still massaging his crotch, which was hard now, fully hard, and so was mine. He looked right at it. "About just wanting to get my dick wet."

He looked into my eyes. His were so blue. My sister was asleep two rooms away. Joey was close to me, and our cocks were straining for each other, whether I wanted them to or not. It was just...happening.

He reached out his hand, brushed his fingertips up my

74

smooth side. He took my hand and brought it to his crotch. My stomach was in my throat. I let my hand rest against the fabric of his briefs, feeling the heat there, the hardness. "I know you want to," he said, and he was so close to me now. My cock was sticking right out in front of me and nearly touching his.

I grabbed his cock through his underwear. It was so hard.

Joey let out his breath. He gripped my lower back, pulled my body closer to him. "I want it, too," he said, and I took my hand away as he pushed our bodies together, our hard dicks mashing up against one another. I looked in his eyes, and he was looking right at me with lust, and I recognized the look because it mirrored what I was feeling.

We kissed. I don't know if he kissed me or I kissed him. We just came together, and then I was letting it all go. His tongue went into my mouth and mine into his. I grabbed hold of his shoulders, fell into his body. He grabbed my ass, hard. We pushed our hard dicks against one another, humping as we made out, our tongues fighting for space in each other's mouths, the taste of beer and cigarettes and *him*.

Where my sister's tongue has been.

I broke away from him. "We can't," I whispered.

Joey glanced at the closed bedroom door. "Let's go out to my car," he said.

Did I have second thoughts as Joey slowly, quietly, opened the front door? As I followed him outside into the bright moonlight, my bare feet on the still-warm concrete steps that led to the driveway? The night air was comfortable, the sound of crickets and cicadas like a refrain. I may have told myself that the damage was already done, that it could just be a one-time thing. I may not have been thinking at all.

I was just following Joey's tight butt into that rambling, sexy car.

Was my sister dreaming as Joey opened the door to the back seat and ushered me inside? I imagined her dreaming of numbers, responsibilities, the future. I remember spending the night at my grandparents' when we were kids, me and her and some cousins, and we couldn't sleep. "Let's make an itinerary for tomorrow!" she had said. The first on the list was, "Splash cold water on our faces." That had been her identity even then, and I'd been the messy one, the one who did things like what I was doing right now.

There wasn't any going back as Joey slid into the back seat of the car next to me and carefully shut the door. The moon shone through the back window, and I settled into the deep, soft seat. Joey put his hands on my sides. For a moment, he regarded my body, running his hands down my smooth sides and across my chest and stomach.

"I've never done it with a guy before," he said.

"Really?" I said.

"You're so hot, though."

I wondered if I reminded him of her, the tightness of our bodies, our pale skin.

He took off my shorts. I raised my ass to help. My hard cock bounded out, sprang upward. He tossed the shorts to the floor and, to my surprise, leaned down and took my cock in his mouth. Tentatively, he suckled the head of it. Then he let his breath out through his nose and sank his mouth all the way down.

I was barely breathing, but this made me groan. He drew his mouth upward, keeping a tight suction, and now he was tasting it fully, using his rough tongue to coat my shaft and darting the tip of it into my piss slit. I could see his cock, still hard in his briefs, a wet spot at the front. He brought his hand to his cock and shifted so that he could stroke himself as he sucked. He groaned his enjoyment as he bobbed his head on my cock. I was close, so I backed away from him. He got the message and came off of my cock.

He wiped the back of his hand across his mouth. I was lying along the seat, and he was in between my legs. He put his hand on the back of my head and leaned forward to kiss me. I stroked his cock through his briefs as we kissed, then slipped my fingers into the top of them and pulled them down over his cock.

"Oh, fuck yeah," he said into my sloppy mouth as I stroked his bare cock. He helped me slide his underwear over his thighs and he kicked them off his feet. There was his cock, in the moonlight, hard as wood, pale and white as the rest of him, the head a girlish shade of pink. I practically had to pry it away from his stomach. It was somewhat bigger than mine, well-proportioned, in a thatch of light brown hair with a big set of balls that hung low between his thighs.

He sat back and I got between his legs. I licked up the shaft, then took the whole thing in my mouth, sliding it down my throat like a stripper on a pole. The smell from him was musky, deep. I recognized it from working in the attic with him—the smell of straight boy, most of it emanating from his pubes. I buried my nose in them, savored it as his cock pulsed in my mouth. When I slid back up, I tasted his pre-come, salty and tart. I wanted more. I wanted his seed, wanted to suck it out of his nuts and swallow it down.

"I was so horny lying in bed with her," he said as I sucked him. The sound of his voice was deadened by the close quarters of the car. "All I could think about was you."

This nearly made me come. I was stroking my own cock as I sucked him on all fours, my ass spread out behind me. I could feel my asshole, exposed to the air. I wanted all of him in me. I wanted him to take me completely. I wanted to do anything for this fucking stud who'd conquered my sister and was now conquering me.

"I'm gonna come," he said. "You gonna take it?"

"Mm hm," I said around his cock. I cupped his balls in my hand, sucking tight with my mouth and stroking myself at the same time. I was getting close, too.

"You gonna swallow for me? You know she won't, right?"

I didn't know that. Maybe I didn't want to know. I kept my head bobbing, his cock hitting the back of my throat. I felt his nuts scrunch up, felt the dome underneath them swelling.

"She won't, but you will, right? Fuck, I'm gonna come. Oh fuck. Ah!"

Hot come flooded my mouth. I sucked him deep and held it there, feeling his cock pulsate, each shot of come more voluminous than the next. Some guys come a lot, I've come to know. Joey came like a geyser. I couldn't believe how much come was flooding my throat. I swallowed and swallowed some more.

"Take it. Oh fuck, take it," he moaned.

I was coming, too. I let go of his balls and cupped my hand in front of my cock, trying to aim my wad into my palm as I swallowed Joey's seed.

When he was done, Joey took the sides of my head and brought my face to his. He kissed me deeply, his tongue probing my mouth as if he were hungry for the taste of himself. I held my wad in my hand. Joey saw it and brought my hand to his mouth. He lapped the come out of my palm like a cat at a bowl of milk, then he came back to me and shared my load with me, the two of us making out in a come-sloppy tongue kiss.

This was something I'd never done before, a level of abandon and raw nastiness that was straight out of a porno movie. But it turned me on like crazy. We were licking and sucking each other's faces as if ravenous for any vestiges of one another's loads.

He laid back against the seat, rested his head on the window, his eyes directed at the stars, his chest heaving. I sat beside him.

"I got some on your seat," I said.

He waved a hand. "I'll clean it up tomorrow."

"Do you think it'll leave a stain?"

Joey took a deep breath. He leaned forward slowly, like he didn't care to look at it, but did it to appease me. It was just a few spots, each no bigger than the size of a dime, slick and pearlescent in the moonlight. My seed, my come, fertilizing the back seat of his car. "I don't know," Joey said and rubbed his thumb into them, swiping up what he could. He popped the thumb into his mouth, sucking off what he'd gathered as he flopped back on his back. "I guess we'll find out."

79

9

Let me tell you about guilt. It's an emotion I came to know well over the rest of the summer. Guilt that stuck to me like sweat, streamed into my eyes salty hot. Guilt that made a home in my stomach, a dull, sickly throb. Guilt like an adrenaline shot to the heart, sending me into a frenzy of fear.

But right then, as we put on our shorts and left the car (Joey pushing the door shut so gently, a quiet click as it latched into place), it was just a shiver. Joey went into the house first. Really, it had only taken ten, fifteen minutes to completely upend my life as I knew it. Not a lot of time at all.

A shiver, like when you're swimming in a lake and hit a cold patch of water and realize you don't know what's going on under the murky depths of it. You wonder what could be living under there, what could brush against your legs, bite your toes, creep inside your bathing suit....

Joey went into the bathroom. I sat on the couch. A shiver, slight enough that I could pass it off, focus on the television, which had been on the whole time, oblivious, now in commercials, a fresh-faced black girl saying you could have a career, the perfect time to enroll was now, call now.

Joey was in the bathroom, and I was alone and had nothing to do but fall asleep, which wasn't going to happen. What was I going to do? What had I just done?

Joey came out. Stood there for a moment, awkwardly looked at the TV, shifted on his legs. I wanted him to sit with me, to talk about what we would do now, to explain things, help me make sense.

Or maybe we could drive away? I thought. *Just pick up and leave it all....*

"Night," he said and went into the bedroom. I heard the hum of the fan as he opened the door, saw the sleeping figure of my sister on the bed. He shut the door. He was in the bedroom, I was on the couch, both of us were back where we were supposed to be. But my mind wasn't. It had been rearranged and replaced.

He was in my sister's bedroom and I was on the couch and that was how it was.

I don't remember falling asleep. I woke up to the sound of Trisha washing dishes. My eyes were gooey with the sticky stuff that hardens in the corners of your eyes. I rubbed it out with the back of my hand, sat up to see her standing next to the sink in her high heels.

It was Monday. She was wearing her power suit, her hair brushed out, long and soft and resting on her collar, the severity of her shoes and suit put off by her hair and the way she stood, dutifully doing the dishes I'd left the night before. Two beer bottles were rinsed and draining in the rack, ready for the recycling bin.

I did something bad last night. The words in my brain. The shiver of guilt. I took a deep breath. I put on a T-shirt.

"Hey," I said. She didn't hear me. I stood up and went to

the kitchen.

"Good morning," she said, smiling, going about her task. I sat on the kitchen chair. She was humming. She was in a good mood.

I said, "Thanks for doing the dishes. I was going to do them."

She didn't say anything and I couldn't see her face, but I imagined her rolling her eyes. If I was going to do the dishes, why *hadn't* I?

I am a horrible person.

"Did Mom call you?" she said.

"No."

"She called me, like, three times. She wants us to come over for dinner tonight."

"Oh," I said.

"Yep. Cabbage rolls."

"Oh, *no.*"

Trisha laughed. "She really can't cook, can she? The last time she made those cabbage rolls, the rice was, like, pouring out. Overcooked into oblivion," she said.

"It wasn't even rice anymore."

"It was...custard." She looked back at me, laughed as I laughed with her, her red hair falling over her face. *I am a horrible person. I am a horrible person.* "But you ate, like, five of them!"

"I can't help it. I go into a food guilt addiction status when I'm there and eat whatever she puts in front of me," I said.

"I know. It's like her form of punishment for us not spending enough time with her. Oh, also, our cousin is getting

82

married. Dustin. The wedding's in three weeks. So, I guess you need to get a suit or something."

"I have one. Somewhere. Do I need to get a gift?" I said.

"I'll just get something from all of us."

"I guess I could get it."

She looked back at me. "Why?" she said.

"I don't know. Never mind." I'm not sure why I suggested it, but it did occur to me that I was just as capable of going into a store and buying something from a gift registry as my sister, and that maybe neither she nor my mother thought of me as being able to do such a task.

But then I was already proving myself capable of things my sister would never suspect.

If, over the next few months, guilt was running laps around my brain, lust was always waiting at the bend, ready to grab the baton. Sometimes they ran neck and neck, and if you think this was exhausting, crazy-making, you'd be correct.

As soon as my sister left that morning, lust was fresh out of the gate and in it to win it.

I watched her leave, the just-rising sun glinting off the navy-blue body of her Toyota. A sensible car. We'd both got some money from our dad when we turned eighteen, remnants of royalties from his book. Trish had bought her car. I'd used it to buy, oh, maybe fifty to a hundred ounces of weed over my four years of college.

I had to work that night at five, and Joey didn't work until five most days, which was around the same time Trisha got home from work.

How convenient....

I stood at the window, watching the sun coming up over the trees, the valley glowing with sultry, early light, the promise of a summer day with nothing to do. And Joey.

I had a boner, hard and throbbing in the same shorts I'd been wearing last night. Guilt told me to go jack off, and I was almost ready to go to the bathroom and take care of business when Joey came out of the bedroom.

If I was feeling like I'd spent the night in a restless haze, Joey looked as fresh and well-slept as a cat stretching out in a patch of sunlight. He rubbed his eyes, revealing the brush of damp hair in his armpits.

"Morning," he said. He was still wearing underwear, but a different pair this time—white boxer briefs with legs that hugged his thick thighs, the crotch chock full of his prick and nuts, a single blue button on the fly. He smiled when my eyes made their way back to his face. "Were you gonna use the bathroom?" he said.

I moved my hand from the side of the door. "Uh, you can use it."

He walked toward me, looked at my crotch. I looked down. I was half hard, my hard-on tenting out the front of my underwear.

"You sure you don't need to use it first?" he said.

I shook my head, turned away.

"All right. I'm gonna take a shower." He strode into the bathroom and shut the door.

84

I decided to get dressed. I was keeping all my stuff behind the easy chair. I had two luggage bags of clothes, but basically they were empty, with a giant pile of clothes on top of them. I threw on a pair of shorts. The shower came on just as I was heading to the back door.

I went outside and stepped through the damp grass, which needed to be mowed, sidled up to a tree, and pulled out my cock, which was as hard as ever. I didn't know how I was going to piss through it.

I took a breath, and another.

Pack up your things, go to Mom's. My pee started to flow, a thick warm stream that splattered in the still-low sunshine.

But I'd have to walk with my bags. And how would I explain to Trisha just suddenly splitting? That would probably make me seem more guilty. And fuck, what if Joey decided to tell her? But that doesn't seem likely.

Joey hadn't seemed bothered by it at all. And maybe it wasn't such a big deal. If he didn't care, why should I?

Besides, she did the same thing to you in high school.

What I did was go back inside and clean up my clothes, folding them and separating the dirty from the clean, throwing them in the washing machine along with some of Trisha's and Joey's laundry because I was a good brother who acted good. (And did I take a sniff of a pair of Joey's dirty underwear? No, I didn't.) I resolved to make less of a mess around the house. I grabbed the broom and swept the kitchen floor, and I was filling up the mop bucket when Joey finished his shower.

I saw the door to the bathroom open, then he came around it. He faced me, rubbing his closely-shorn head with a brown towel, fluffing it against his face. He was completely naked, and as he moved the towel, his fully-erect cock bounced between his legs like a puppy begging for a treat.

"You work today?" he said, beginning to walk toward me. *Bouncy, bouncy, bouncy....*

"Uh, yeah. At five, like usual." I turned off the faucet and the mop water steamed in my face. Joey walked past me and reached up to open a cabinet. He pulled down a box of Captain Crunch and poured it into a bowl. When I looked over at him, I saw his hard dick laying on the counter.

I poured pine cleaner into the water and was hauling the bucket to the floor as Joey came around me, his boner just inches from my body as he maneuvered to the fridge and got the milk. "Just one sec," he said, watching me grab the mop. "Be right out of your way." He poured his milk (but didn't put the milk away) and stepped out of the kitchen. Stood in the doorway, took a bite of cereal. "Wanna help me in the attic? I'm gonna set up my stereo and speakers."

I looked at him. It looked like his cock was going down. It looked like a deflating bicycle tire draped over his fuzzy nuts. I tried to ignore my persistent half hard-on, though Joey kept glancing at it.

"Yeah, sure," I said.

Joey nodded and walked into the bedroom. Tight little bubble butt, lightly hairy cheeks that flexed with each step.... He shut the door.

I finished mopping and went down to the basement to change the laundry.

◆

I folded clothes on the couch. My suitcases were basically packed.

I need to lay the groundwork first. Tell Mom it's not working out, move back in with her, tell Trisha it's because I don't want to pay rent anymore, and besides, Mom needs me....

Joey came out of the bedroom wearing clothes this time. No boner visible, which was a relief.

"Nice of you to clean up," he said. "Trish will appreciate it."

I had to sit down. I pulled my knees to my chest.

"You alright?" he said.

"I think so. How are you?"

"Great," he said. He looked great. He looked completely unbothered, in fact, and a quick, bizarre notion floated up: *Maybe it hadn't happened? Maybe it was a dream?*

"To be honest, I'm freaked out," I said.

"Yeah?" he said, like he never would've guessed, like we weren't just sucking each other's come off our tongues six or so hours earlier.

"Yeah. You're not?"

Joey shifted on his feet, looked up toward the ceiling. "I don't know.... No, not really. I mean, like I said, I never did nothing like that with a guy before. But it was cool," he said, shrugging, a smile going across his face. Fuck, he was adorable.

"Well...what about, you know, the fact that I'm your girlfriend's brother?"

He scrunched up his mouth, tilted his head. Like he had to

think about it for a second. "It bothers you?" he said.

"A little," I said, exasperated.

Joey got a worried look. "Are you gonna say something?"

"God, no. Are you?"

"Fuck no."

"Good," I said. *Was it good?*

"So...."

"I just feel guilty, you know?"

Joey sat on the easy chair and lit a cigarette. I watched him suck it back, his elbow raised at a ninety-degree angle as he held the cigarette to his mouth. He regarded me through squinted eyes, exhaled, the smoke clouding his face. "Don't feel guilty," he said. "It was just fooling around. Nobody has to know. We can do whatever we want and nobody has to know. It's just between us."

I let out my breath. Lust had taken up the baton again. Or maybe guilt was just exhausted and chilling in the shade somewhere.

My blood succumbed to gravity, sank to my pelvis, congested capillaries in my cock and asshole. "Let me have a hit of that cigarette," I said and took it from him. Our fingers entangled as he passed it to me, the most natural, comfortable thing. I took a puff.

Joey got up and sat next to me. I handed back the cigarette. Our thighs touched.He wrapped his hand around the back of my neck, squeezed it. It felt good, better than good. I closed my eyes. Joey moved his hand down my back, lightly massaging my muscles, tight and clenched from sleeping on the cramped sofa.

I couldn't remember the last time I'd been touched like this, had received physical affection. No, I could: It was with Eric, my boyfriend in college. For the first few weeks, we were sleeping together every night, curled up, always touching. Then it had tapered off. Then the sex had tapered off, too, and we broke up before my senior year.

Feeling Joey's hand made me realize the intense comfort in having somebody touch you. My family wasn't affectionate. My mom would always hug and kiss us, but it was like she did it out of duty, to throw it in my dad's face, who was very uncomfortable with touch. The time Trisha had held me after Dad died had been a one-time thing. Touch made us all anxious for some reason.

"Feel better?" he said around the cigarette.

"Yeah, I do," I said,

He took his hand away from my neck. "Come help me up in the attic."

10

That attic. It was practically a secret itself, the way the door was so tiny and hidden.

Joey led me through the bedroom. I noticed something new on her dresser, a ceramic pot filled with bright-red soy wax that sat over a votive—some aromatherapy thing. It seemed to be cherry-chocolate scented.

Joey opened the attic door and I followed up him the stairs. It was hot up there. The rough wooden floor and exposed beams seemed to add to the heat. Joey had cleaned off the pullout sofa we'd found up there, spread blankets over it. The light from the front window was bright and filled the room. Joey put the fan in the window and turned it on.

"I already brought it up here," Joey said, indicating stereo components in a pile on the floor. "We just gotta set it up."

So we did, and as we did, things started to seem normal, and I thought maybe I could just pretend like nothing ever happened. But, at the same time, Joey was sweating near me and his cock was flopping around in his shorts and I wanted to suck it again. I wanted to feel his body on mine and do everything we'd done last night and more.

I opened a box that was labeled "CDs." Half of it was CDs and the other half was porno DVDs. Joey saw me looking and came over. His head hovered over my shoulder. I could smell him.

"Wanna watch one?" he said. I was kneeling on the floor.

He pressed his crotch against my shoulder and I could feel his cock getting hard.

I stood. "We better not," I said, but I didn't sound convincing. Joey put a hand on my back and another on my chest, rubbed my sternum.

"C'mon, man. I know you're horny. You had a boner first thing this morning. I usually jack off in the shower, but I didn't this morning because I wanted to save it for you." He moved his hand down my stomach, grabbed my dick. I got hard, fast.

It wasn't like I could deny it. I could've pushed his hand away. I didn't. One more time. Why not? It would just go into the same place, a bank of guilt and shame, stored right next to the last experience.

"You saw me when I came out of the shower. You know what got me so hard? I was thinking about what we did last night. Did you like that?"

I put my hand behind me, placed it on the hard cock in his shorts. "Yes," I said.

"You like looking at me naked?" I turned to face him and shook my head yes. He stepped back. With a smile, he removed his shirt. Ran his hand up his stomach and across his chest. "I'm not wearing any underwear." He slid off his shorts, stood there in all his glory. "Now you," he said.

I stripped for him. He sat on the sofa and watched. I didn't put on much of a show, but I liked the way he looked at me. He was as turned on by me as I was by him.

When I was done, he stood up and came to me. I felt his smooth chest, his pecs. "Fuck, I love that," he said when I tweaked his nipples. He shivered when I touched his abdomen.

91

"Look how much I'm pre-coming. I never pre-come this much. You're getting me so turned on."

"I am, too," I said, looking down at the pearl of pre-come on the tip of my dick. Joey reached down and used his finger to swipe it off my cock, then brought the drop to his mouth and ate it.

"Mm," he said. "Try mine." I did the same. It tasted fantastic. "You can have it whenever you want, you know. You turn me on so bad, it's crazy." He milked my dick like a toothpaste tube and brought another dollop of pre-come out, which he put on his tongue. Then he kissed me, letting me taste myself, backing off and swiping more off his cock and pushing it into my mouth, kissing me some more. "You and me, we're come brothers," he said.

"Come brothers," I said, chuckling.

"Yeah," he said, looking in my eyes.

I kissed him like I was starving. I was gone completely. "Fuck, Joey."

He lay down on the floor and I climbed on top of him, my crotch in his face and his in mine. We sixty-nined, sucking each other's cocks in the hot attic, a sheen of sweat forming on our bodies. The pleasure of sucking Joey's hard prick was amplified by the pleasure of him taking mine into his soft mouth. I kept my hips hovered above his face so that I wouldn't choke him, but he seemed comfortable with it buried down his throat as deeply as possible and raised his head from the floor to get it all the way inside, choking on it a few times, but in it to win it. I did the same.

I knew we were gonna come at the same time. Joey took

hold of my balls, so I did the same thing, gently squeezing his fuzzy nuts in my hand, feeling them scrunch up as his orgasm approached. I heard his muffled groans increase, both of us sucking cock like it was something we were born to do, until I tasted the first shot of his load in my mouth and, a few moments later, the tight suction Joey had on my cock made me lose it, too, both of us blowing our loads into each other's mouths and swallowing them down.

Just as I was starting to finish coming, Joey grabbed my waist, pulled me around to him, and kissed me, our come-sloppy tongues mingling just as they had the night before.

Then I lay next to him, the grime on the carpet grinding into my sweaty skin as I heaved and caught my breath.

Joey turned to me. "I love that you're just as freaky as I am," he said.

◆

I'll give this to myself: I left early for work. I could've stuck around for another hour, in fact. That's something, right?

After we set up the stereo, I went downstairs and took a shower, and when I got out, Joey was watching TV on the sofa, my sofa, and he was still buck naked, his back resting on my pillow and one leg on the floor so that his soft cock hung invitingly, unavoidably, a constant invitation. He was still sweaty from our sex earlier, and I wondered if I would smell him on my pillow that night, the musk of his pits, the alpha male marking his territory.

I got dressed. Sat on the couch next to him and watched TV

for a while. He suggested getting high, but I didn't want to. I felt like the high would just amplify everything, would make me way too crazy.

I thought of his ass when I'd seen him that morning, walking naked into the bedroom, his cheeks tight and muscular. I thought of eating it, of asking him to take a shower so he'd be squeaky clean, maybe taking a shower with him, sliding all over each other's bodies, eating his clean ass with water flowing down the valley of his back like a river, fresh and thick on my face as I tongue-fucked his hole....

I knew he'd do it if I asked. I got the sense that he was up for just about anything.

"I'm gonna head out," I said.

"Work?"

"Yeah."

"Seems early."

"I've got to help my mom with something before I go in," I said, but I didn't. I just needed to get out of the house, to give myself some space to think.

I entered the porn store to find the mannequin that modeled our lingerie (cheap and sold in paper packages) on the floor. We called her Sylvia, and she was topless now, with scuffs on her face. Randy was bent over her, and he looked up as I walked in.

"What happened?" I said.

"Rape and murder," Randy said, hoisting up his pants. "Perp wore a strap-on."

"Ooh, Elliot Stabler," I said.

"Don't you want to just climb him like a tree?" Randy said.

I laughed and set my bag down behind the counter,

94

clocked in. Randy was stripping the mannequin of her fishnet stockings. One of the magazine shelves was in disarray, with half of them in piles on the floor next to boxes of penis-shaped pasta and buttercream-flavored massage butter. "What's going on in here?" I said.

Randy picked up the mannequin. "I knocked her over. She fell on her face. Knocked her arms off, too."

"I think you put them on backwards," I said.

"Oh, for fuck's sake. Well, I'll let you take care of that."

"No problem," I said, coming around the counter. "What's with all the stuff on the floor?"

"I'm getting rid of it. All those magazines. Three packs of titles that haven't been published in five years! And that bachelorette party shit? Nobody comes in here for bachelorette parties. All that crap was here when I bought the store, and I swear it's been collecting dust ever since. I'm gonna buy books, I think. Or nice, quality toys. I'm over this place!" he said, throwing up his arms.

"Are you okay?" I said.

"Yeah. I'm okay. You know, I bought this place after Dom died, and I haven't done anything with it since. It's making okay money, but I don't care. I don't even need the money. So I've decided to do whatever the fuck I want with it. How about that?" he said and swiped an armful of tiaras with cocks on them onto the floor.

"All right," I said.

"Plus, last week was the anniversary of his death. I guess I'm just feeling like it's time for a change."

I switched Sylvia's arms and got a rag to try and clean off

95

her face.

"So, what's up with you?" Randy said, looking at me. "You look...washed out."

I took a deep breath. I had no doubt that he was right. Washed out, spun out, my nuts having been emptied twice into my sister's boyfriend in the last fourteen hours, while I had a belly full of his come.

Randy asked, "You getting enough sleep?"

"For the most part."

"You ain't smokin' that *dope* are you?" he said, leaning into me.

"Maybe sometimes," I said.

"I knew it!" Randy said. "You gotta hook me up sometime. It's been years."

"Definitely," I said, thinking of how fun it would be to toke up with my boss. "You're crazy," I said.

"I know. I don't care. This is *my* store. I can do whatever I want. Fuck it all!" he screamed.

Lloyd poked his head out from the entrance of the arcade, glanced at us through his brown, bottle-thick specs, then disappeared back into the darkness.

Randy and I laughed. "There's gonna be some changes around here," he said. "One way or the other. But, for tonight, I need you to enter all those DVDs into the computer."

"Yes, captain," I said.

It was a relief to be at work, to have activities and people to distract me. Randy liked for me to sell stuff, but he didn't want me to be pushy about it. But this businessman-looking guy came in, frail and whiter than white, in Dockers and a button-down shirt, and bought over three hundred dollars in interracial DVDs, which was just bizarre.

Some ladies came in and bought vibrators. They looked for a while at these stupid "porn for women" movies we have with white, gauzy covers, but they didn't buy one. I always put those movies on the in-store monitors because they made me laugh. Our biggest selling DVDs were these celebrity and TV-show-spoofing movies like *The Gang-Bang Theory* and *Hannah Does Montana*.

It hadn't been a busy night, but I'd stayed occupied. That turned into feeling sort of frantic as my shift ended and I prepared to go home to Trisha's. I pulled down several shelves filled with tiny bottles of lube and wiped off each one individually. I mopped the floor, cleaned the parking lot. I was a cleaning machine.

My conscience was the one thing I couldn't scrub with a sponge, and by the time the night guy, Elton, came in to relieve me, it was becoming harder to ignore.

I passed through the woods behind the store to the railroad tracks. It was a dark night, the moon obscured by clouds, and the loneliness of it hit me first. Then it started to seem like everything was unreal. I was going home, and I thought of what home meant, and that's when it hit me. My breath got shallow. I stopped in my tracks, on the tracks, clutching my chest and staring at nothing, paralyzed by the horror of it. I'd never had a panic attack before, but this felt close to one.

I have to tell her. I can't tell her. I'll go to Mom's. I'll leave tonight.

I turned around and started walking toward Mom's. I got halfway there, then turned back around again. I didn't know what the fuck I was doing. Mom would be asleep and would freak the fuck out if I wandered into the house at one in the morning.

They're going to find out eventually. There's no going back.

But I did go back, to my sister's, and by the time I got there, my panic had been replaced by a heavy weariness. I was worn the fuck out.

They were asleep. I crashed on the couch.

Somebody was shaking me. Was I dreaming? I smelled him first. Then I opened my eyes and he was there beside me, his face barely visible in the dark. He knelt beside the sofa.

"Nate!" he whispered.

"What? What's happening?"

"In the attic. After she leaves." His breath was sweet, with a hint of cigarettes. He held my face, his mustache curling as he smiled. "You understand? Meet me up there."

I nodded. I didn't know if I understood. Then he was gone, into the bathroom, and I fell back asleep.

But when I woke up again later, he was still there. He took me by the hand and led me into the bedroom.

"Did Trish leave?" I said, but he didn't say anything, just smiled as we went through the bedroom door. I saw her figure in the bed and panicked—was he going to take me right past her? But it was just the bunched-up sheet. My cock was hard and he took it into his hand, smiling as he led me through the little door up to the attic. We stopped on the stairs halfway up and began to kiss, at first tentative, then intensely making out, our hard-ons pressed together under our shorts.

Then I felt something shift. I looked down the stairs. Trisha was there. She stood stock-still in the doorway. Her hair was a nest of black that covered most of her face, but not her eyes. Her eyes gleamed in the darkness, staring right at me, but they were cold and dead.

The shock of it woke me up. A dream. The sunlight was coming in through the window. I heard a car head down the driveway—Trish's car, leaving. I'd slept through her getting ready.

Trisha standing in that dark-attic stairway was burned like an afterimage in my brain. A nightmare. I laid there trying to excise it from my mind. The sunlight was getting brighter. I heard a creak. Steps.

The steps to the attic. Joey.

11

Blood, thick, shifting from my brain to that old familiar place. The floorboards creaked above me. I lay there, breath coming faster now, cock waking up in my lap, wondering what he was doing up there.

Whump, whump, whump. Three thumps on the floor, in a row, unmistakable for anything else. I took a deep breath and stood. The door to the bedroom was closed. I opened it and went inside. I saw the sheets on the bed, but it didn't look like there was anybody laying there. I imagined it was still warm from Joey's body. The morning light filtered through the curtains, giving the room a dusky red glow.

The attic doorway was open. Light filtered down the wooden stairs from the room above, also TV noises. I started up the stairs, then turned to look behind me, but nobody was there. As I ascended, the sounds got clearer: sex sounds. Porn.

Joey lay back on the couch with one hand propping up his head. He was naked and stroking his hard cock. He smiled at me.

"Morning," he said. Straight porn played on the TV—a woman in pigtails getting railed on both ends by two fat cocks.

I just had my underwear on and my cock was hard. Joey's smile got bigger as I took them off and walked over to him, boner leading the way. His skin glowed in the dusty shafts of morning light, his brown pubes lit up golden.

He reached for my cock as I went to him, so I stood next to

his head and he slid his mouth down my cock. It felt so good. He moaned around it, like he loved the taste, his eyes closed, arching his hips upward as he stroked himself.

I touched his head, felt all over it, the soft fluff of his buzz cut. I passed my palm over his eyes, traced my finger over his mustache and sucked-in cheeks, feeling my cock pass underneath them. The fuzz on his jawline, his throat and neck. His tight stomach. The hairy mound just before the root of his cock. I took hold of his cock, jacked it slowly as he sucked me. God, he was horny, his body undulating against my touch.

I climbed on top of him and went in for a kiss. We sucked each other's tongues in the lazy heat of the attic, and for all the world it was like we were making love, pressing our slick cocks against each other and pressing our bodies impossibly close. Joey kneaded my ass, then slipped his cock between my thighs so that it was riding against my hole.

"I wanna fuck you," he said in my ear. I pushed my ass back against his cock, tensed and released my hole against his shaft. It'd been a while since I'd gotten fucked—not since Eric, actually, so over a year—but right then I wanted it more than I'd ever wanted it from anybody. I wanted him to take me, make me his.

But first I wanted to taste all of him. I started at his neck and licked and sucked down his body, nipples, bellybutton. Skipped his cock and went to his balls, which hung loose and heavy in the heat. I was like a dog lapping at water from a hose, licking each nut up into my mouth, rolling it around. I drew the tip of my tongue along his shaft, salty and sweaty from *I didn't know what*, but preferred not to imagine. I pushed my ass

101

back and up into the air as I sucked his cock down to the root, savoring the taste, my own cock bobbing in my lap. I licked down lower, under his nuts.

"Whoa," Joey moaned, so I kept licking lower. When my tongue flirted with the edge of his musky asshole, Joey shuddered and his knees went up to his chest.

"Oh my god," he said as I went directly for his asshole, licking around and darting my tongue inside the slick, wrinkled muscle. "Oh fuck, lick my ass."

I loved Joey's ass. He had these pertly muscled cheeks, lightly furred, a thicker line of hair running down into his crack and around his pink slot. I savored it all, enjoying Joey's moans and squirms when I shoved my tongue in him as deep as it could go.

"Hold on," he said, and flipped over onto all fours, spreading his cheeks out toward me. Man, that made my cock hard. I made a feast of his ass, and Joey loved every minute of it, lowering his chest to the couch and pushing his ass back like a horny cat. I spread him as wide as I could, buried my face in him. Ducked underneath and took his cock into my mouth, making him gasp as I licked down his shaft, up his nuts, over the dome of his taint and back to his hole.

I was stroking him and thinking he might be getting close when he stopped me. He flipped onto his back and threw his legs up over his head, his cock pointing at his face. "Lick me again. I wanna come like this."

I ate his ass while Joey jacked himself off. It didn't take him long to come, and I watched it, my face peeking over his cheeks, his hole clenching around my tongue as a strong, thick shot of load spurted out of his cock and landed across his face. The next three spurts went right into his open mouth. When he was finished, he pulled me to him, and we shared his load, the taste of his ass and cock, as I jacked off and shot a load that splattered across my chest.

I propped myself up on one end of the couch and Joey set himself up on the other. Our legs were entwined, our soft cocks resting on our nuts. Joey stretched out, his abs elongating as he arched his back. His foot went in between my legs and he wiggled his toes against my nuts.

"That's the second rimjob I've ever got. And the first time, it wasn't anywhere near that good," he said.

"Thanks. It's hot." I thought to ask him who'd given him the first one, but changed my mind.

"I wanna just stay in and fuck all day. Fuck the day away," he said. From the TV came the unconvincing sounds of a filmed female orgasm. Guilt crept up.

"You've really never done this before?" I said.

"No. I mean, I've gotten blowjobs from guys before."

"From who?"

"This one guy in junior high. He sucked my dick a couple times."

"Where?"

"In his backyard. He had a treehouse. He was cool, I guess, but everybody made fun of him. That was it."

"What about, like, cheating on your girlfriend?"

Joey drew his feet away. Shrugged.

"Have you had girlfriends before?" I said.

"Yeah. That's actually why I broke up with my last

103

girlfriend. She caught me with another girl. That girl was nuts, though. She'd come around all time. Girls get, like, attached." He smirked. "That's why this is great. I know you're not gonna get crazy about it. Plus, she's your sister."

I took a deep breath. Had I signed some unholy pact? The sex of my dreams in exchange for my sister? Joey and I were bound now, our lives held together by a secret, a lie. And yes, there was something hot about that. The fact that nobody could know but us. Me and him. "Guy stuff." Getting our rocks off. Doing what we needed to do.

My cock started to rise again. Joey moved his toes back to my balls, then moved them downward to where they flirted with my asshole.

"C'mon, admit it. It's perfect," he said.

"I've never had sex this good."

Joey's cock was getting hard again, too. "Me neither," he said. "It's cause you're just as horny as I am." He came over to my side, raised my legs up, and rested them on his shoulders. He laid his cock against my asshole, pressed against it, dragged his shaft up and down. "Can I fuck you today?"

"We can try."

"You want it, though, don't you?"

"Yeah."

"Say it."

"I want it."

"You want what?"

"I want your cock in me."

"You want me to fuck you like I fuck your sister?"

Jesus. I nodded.

104

"Say it," he said.

"I want you to fuck me like you fuck my sister."

Joey's mouth descended on mine, his hard cock humping against my ass fast and rough, gliding along my sweaty skin, sweat sticking us together. He reared back, let the head of his cock rest against my hole, pressed inward. I felt the pressure of it, like a thumb against the soft spot of an apple. Not going in, yet.

"Do I have to wear a rubber like I do with her?"

"No," I said.

"Oh, fuck yeah," Joey said, leaning down to kiss me again, his cock insistent against my hole. "Fuck you raw."

"I want you to come in me. I want you to breed me."

"Right now?"

"Let's take a shower first."

The cooler air hit my naked body as we descended the attic stairs. In the bathroom, Trish had put a white wicker shelf next to the sink and it held girly toiletries—lotions, exfoliants, makeup, sponges. Joey grabbed a black bag off the bottom shelf. It was crusted with caked-on soap or toothpaste. He unzipped it and pulled out a bottle of lube. Shot me a smile. My knees went weak.

Eric had so far been the only person to fuck me. I know that might sound surprising, but the fact of the matter is that I'm a pretty monogamous person, and bottoming to me always seemed like a big deal. But Eric had convinced me, and I got off on it like nothing else. I let him fuck me pretty much the entire time we were together, and even when I jerked off around that time, I would come with my finger up my ass because I was so attuned to the feeling.

I'd mostly ignored my ass in the year since, but Joey made me remember.

I got in the shower. The water was just cool enough to be refreshing. I reached past Trish's pink shower puff and grabbed the bar of Dial soap I'd bought for myself from the grocery store. I think Joey was using the same bar of soap when he showered. I was lathering up when Joey stepped in.

The shower was white and the curtain was translucent. The bathroom was small, but the light from the window made it glow brightly. Joey looked fresh in the light, his round eyes radiating blue. He got under the spray and swished it across the nub of his head, the light catching the water flicking off of the bristles of his hair. He held out his hand and I handed him the soap. "Don't drop it," I said.

"You're *gonna* drop it." He soaped up, lathering his pits and coating his pecs, stomach, balls, ass. Our cocks were hard. He soaped it, stroked it, smiling at me. He picked up the pink shower scrubby and ran it over his body, then he flipped me around so that my back was to him and slid his hard soapy cock between my thighs, his hard body pressed against my back. He reached around and caressed my chest with the scrubby. I moved away.

"What?" he said.

"I don't want you to use that."

"Okay...," Joey said and put it back on its little white hook. It was just knowing that it was hers. Plus, the fact that he was using my soap and her sponge, together.... "I'll just use my hands," he said, soaping them up. He slid them down my back, his fingers tracing down my spine to my crack and between my cheeks until they made contact with my hole. I pushed back to meet them.

"Mm," Joey said, pushing his fingers into me. One finger darted inside.

I put my hands on the wall of the shower and stuck my butt out, knowing that it would look good like that, firm and spread out.

"What a hot ass," Joey said.

I felt him brush his cock against it, his cock so hard that it barely moved with him, rigid and ready to pierce into me. I concentrated on relaxing my hole, opening it up.

Joey took my thighs and pulled my body backward so that my ass was under the spray of the shower. The water was cool and sharp on my asshole. Joey knelt and licked up my thighs, then to my smooth asshole. He dug his tongue right into me. He wasn't messing around. Christ, it felt good. He was rimming to get me ready for his cock, immediately pushing his tongue as deep as he could, relaxing me, opening me up. I looked down. He was crouched in the shower, stroking his hard cock as he ate me. "Mm," he said, backing off then diving back in, the smooth spear of his tongue sliding inside of me.

My cock was half-hard and leaking, a familiar feeling for me, since I rarely get hard-ons when I'm getting fucked. It's more like a persistent tumescence where I leak pre-come like crazy.

He opened the curtain and grabbed the lube from the side of the sink. I heard the pop as he uncapped it. He slathered some onto his finger and brought it to my hole, pressing in. I pressed back, and the tip of his finger went in again. It took me a minute to breathe and adjust and allow it in, and Joey kept his finger real still just like I needed him to.

He slid it in another inch, and now I was feeling opened up, so he slid it in all the way to his second knuckle, pressing the tip of it against my prostate, which made me feel so intensely vulnerable. He reached around and stroked my cock while he fingered me until my cock got hard, then he slid a second finger in beside the first one. I felt stretched out, but it felt amazing, like I only wanted more, my ass primed for the taking.

"Fuck yeah," Joey said, pumping his fingers in and out of me. He stood and I felt his rock-hard cock against my slippery wet ass. It was so easy, was the thing. So easy just to slide it in, to fuck away, to give us what we both wanted and damn the consequences. Me, a slippery fucktoy for him to enjoy. He didn't even need to put more lube on me or on him. He just adjusted his cock till the head was next to my hole, pressed against it.

"I'm gonna fuck you right here," he said.

"No, let's go upstairs first." Thinking, *It'd be too easy for her to catch us down here. If we were upstairs, we could hear her coming. We'd have time to hide it.*

"Can I just slide it in? Just once. Then we'll go upstairs." His cock was poised at the precipice. My ass relaxed, ready to gobble it up. "C'mon. Just once."

I didn't say anything, just let his cock press against my hole. I knew I wanted it and I knew he knew I wanted it, but we rested there because we both knew that that was where desire lived, where it was at its most intense, when it hadn't happened yet, when it was a fantasy of itself, a promise yet to be delivered.

"Okay. Just once."

"Say what you want."

"I want your cock inside me."

"Except not like with your sister. Raw."

"Raw," I said, thinking, *I can't be this dirty, this careless, this evil.*

A slight push—me against him or him against me, it was impossible to say—and then the tip of his cock was inside me, and he just kept going, inch after inch of his hard shaft disappearing up my tight asshole until I felt his pubes pressing against my ass.

"Fuck yeah. I'm in you. Christ, you're tight."

I loved it. Loved his cock in me, felt more turned on than I ever had in my life.

"Inside you for the first time," he said in my ear.

We should go upstairs, I thought, but then Joey was sliding out and I didn't want him to slide out.

He paused right before it went out all the way. "You want it again?"

"Yes," I said.

He slammed it this time, the slap of his wet skin against mine.

I cried out, the sound thudding against the flat plastic walls of the shower. "Oh fuck," I said. "Fuck me."

"Yeah?" he said, pulling out a few inches, pausing, then slamming it back in, his balls slapping against my ass, the strength of his hips pushing me forward. "Nobody's gonna catch us," he said, pulling out, back in, fucking me now, fucking my ass. "It's just you and me."

"Fuck me," I said.

"Fuck yeah. Say it again."

"Fuck me."

He kept going, slow and sure, both of us ready to come at a moment's notice, but making it last. It never felt this good, not with Eric, not with anybody.

Joey said, "Tell you what: I only want to come in you."

"What?" I said.

"You're the only one who's gonna get my come. I'll never shoot it in her, not in her mouth or her cunt or ass. Only you'll get it. How's that make you feel?" He started pumping me harder, reached around and started jacking my cock. He licked the back of my neck, nibbling on it. "How's that make you feel?" he said again.

"I want it. I want your come."

"That's right," he said, slamming into me harder. "Fucking take it!"

Harder and harder he fucked me, jacking me off until I was past the point. And what if she came in right then, what if? Opening the bathroom door and seeing me, her brother, getting fucked raw by her boyfriend, fucking like lovers, or maybe fucking like lovers never could?

Joey said, "I'm gonna come in you."

"I'm gonna come, too. Oh fuck!"

"Fuck!" he said, slammed into me hard and held it there. I felt it, hot and spreading inside of me, and it triggered my own orgasm, which I splurted all over the shower, his hand whacking it out of me. I felt like I was totally out of control, everything loose and insane.

He took his cock out of me, let me go. I used my hand to clean up my come, swiped it onto the shower floor. Knelt down to make sure it flowed through the screen on the drain and didn't get stuck in the wad of long, red hair.

I got out and dried off next to him.

"Sorry I came so quick," he said. "I've never been so turned on in my life."

"Me neither," I said.

"You gonna keep it inside you?" he said.

"I guess so."

He reached behind me, shoved a finger up my freshly fucked hole, felt his load in there. When he took out his finger, he popped it into his mouth, sucked it clean. "Mm," he said. "I want you to keep it in as long as you can."

"Okay, Joey."

And then I was alone in the bathroom, putting my shorts back on. But I didn't want it inside me anymore, so I sat on the toilet.

What if she'd come home? For lunch or for any reason?

So, it was the first time he fucked me, but it was also the first time, but not the last, that we got so carried away, so turned on by the danger of it, that we got careless.

This is going to end at some point, I thought. *With a bang and a mess.*

111

12

I had four hours to kill before work so, I went to my mother's cause I didn't know what else to do. The pendulum had swung. I was feeling sick with guilt, and I couldn't sit around with Joey, who was his typical, untroubled self.

My mom wasn't home. I found myself wandering around my empty childhood home, taking it all in, my mind a blank. My sister's old room with its blue and pink wallpaper, trophies on the shelf from cross country and track. I remembered she had built that shelf herself, had, in fact, made Mom drive her to the hardware store to buy supplies to make it. Now it was covered in a thick layer of dust. This seemed unbearably sad to me.

You're fucking her boyfriend, fucking the only guy she's cared enough to live with. It hit me like an anvil to the head, and I crumpled to the carpet and rolled myself up in a ball. I wanted to cry, but I couldn't, just clutched myself in a panic that began to dissipate after a while.

I was going to leave when I passed the basement door. It was shut tight. I opened it. Musty air hit my nose. I flipped on the light and started down.

Mom's basement was seventy-five percent unfinished, except for an area Dad had fixed up as his office. When I was a kid, it had seemed like a labyrinth down there, with cobweb-encrusted passages and rooms where nobody had any business being. When I was five, I had a nightmare that there was a graveyard down there, crumbling stone monuments half-buried in a dirt-floor crawlspace.

Dad's office was in a corner, dry-walled and cozy. There was a desk—really just an old door he'd set across two sawhorses—a lamp on top of that. A rolling office chair about twenty years past its prime. There was a small table, heavy with books. There were books piled in the corners, too, some stacked on top of milk crates and some right on the floor, water-stained and musty: novels, history books, biographies. My dad was a big reader, and that was mostly what he did down here: read. He rarely read upstairs. From what I remembered from the last few years he was alive, he spent most of his time in the basement.

I was looking through his books when I heard Mom come home.

"Who's there?" she said.

"It's me."

"Oh," she said, and I sensed her hesitate before she started down the stairs. "Whatever are you doing down there?" she said, her voice getting louder.

"Just looking around," I said.

She stood next to me and put her hand on my shoulder. "I haven't been down here in ages," she said.

"Me either," I said. I did have a memory of coming down here a week or two after he had died, only to get creeped out and run back upstairs. Another nightmare I had after Dad died: turning a corner in the basement and seeing him sitting at his desk, his back to me, and feeling petrified that he would turn around.

"Why did he spend so much time down here?" I said.

"Who knows?" Mom said. "I'd come down here and catch him writing sometimes, though. In notebooks. He'd get embarrassed. Angry. Always claimed he was done with writing." Mom continued to rub my shoulder. It felt good. "I used to try to push him to write again," she said in a far-off voice. "I thought it might...make things different. You know, I fell in love with him as a writer. His book having some success, not much but enough. Then we got married and *pfft*. That part of him disappeared. Into this basement. Along with the rest of him."

I got this vision of my mother, young, in Pittsburgh, meeting my dad, her whole life ahead of her. Then in this house, pregnant, my dad receding, becoming a shadow.

"I guess he wasn't that good to you," I said, measuring my words. I hated giving her sympathy, doing anything that would support her image of herself as a martyr.

"I could've gotten a lot less," she said, squeezing my neck. "He was good to you kids, or he was in the earlier years. I just don't think he was a man cut out for marriage. Maybe not for being around people, in general. Funny, you're the same age as when I met him."

This had never occurred to me, and for a moment, it was paralyzing. By my age, Dad had already written his book, had done the one thing he would be remembered for, while I'd done shit. I had the worst of him, I thought—the artistic ambition, but not the acumen to pull it off, and just like him, I was alienating myself from my family in more insidious, awful ways. Fucking my sister's boyfriend, bumming around my old

114

hometown, dreaming of artistic success as a way of ignoring the fact that I was going to end up here for the rest of my life, working in a porno store, and never talking to my family again.

"I am glad that neither of you kids wound up like him," she said.

"You don't think I'm like him?"

"Oh no," she said, taking her hand away. I followed her up the stairs. "You care too much. You're there for me. And for your sister." I looked back down one more time, then I switched off the light and shut the door.

"Do you think Joey has something interesting?" Mom said. She'd just made me some food: a sandwich, tomato soup. She stood at the sink, washing the dishes.

My senses pricked up, my defenses. It was the first time I'd ever heard her talk positively about him, and she said it dreamily, slowly, in a savoring way, her hands in the white sudsy dishwater. "Like a...star quality."

"*Star quality*?" I said, trying to sound dismissive, but the catch in my voice was apparent, maybe. My guts rumbled audibly.

She ignored me. "Like a...sexuality," she said.

"Gross," I said, which was a genuine reaction to hear something like that from my mother.

"I mean, he could use a few more brain cells. He's the kind of boy who latches onto something, or else he falls into nothing."

115

"I'm sure they're fine."

"You're the one sharing lives with them," she said. And ordinarily, I would cut into her for that—*sharing lives*, like we're serving one another up on a silver platter, parties every night, outings galore, *our lives as one*. Which is what Mom would want for me—to live with her, to share her life.

But with her hands in the sink and her eyes looking through the same yellowed lace window curtain that had been there since I could remember, it felt scary. Like she knew more than I did.

"Did you know I was a virgin when I got married to your father?"

I looked at the newspaper I was reading, mortified and planning my escape from this kitchen, conversation, life.

"We didn't have sex the whole time we were dating. And then we had your sister not nine months after the wedding."

"C'mon, Mom."

"Oh, don't be a prude," she said, which was rich. "You're the gay one, after all."

"Whatever that means."

"It means I have to picture the things you do in bed—"

"Oh, come *on*."

"I can't help it! I'm just telling you." The silverware clinked as she gathered a bunch in her hand and tossed it into the rack. "Your father and I had a very satisfying sexual relationship the first couple of years. And then it just stopped."

"Why?" I said, unable to repress my curiosity.

"It stopped just like everything did with your father. I think he got easily discouraged. It was just like him to pursue something, get all excited about it, then cease to care once the people caught on to what he was doing. He only liked to live in secret."

I got a glimpse of something going on under the surface, but I didn't pursue it. For obvious reasons. *Like father, like son....*

"With the book, I practically had to hold his hand to sign the royalty checks. He thought it was all a shame, thought the book was terrible. My, how he hated himself," she said, shaking her head and gazing through the window like he was out there looking in on us. "Anyway, something about it—your sister, Joey—reminds me of your father. The way she looks at him."

"Like she's satisfied?" I said.

"Nathan!"

"What, I can't talk about it?"

She smiled. "He's attractive, right?"

"I don't know. I guess so," I said, and she shot me a look over her shoulder, just a glance as she situated a bowl atop the dishes in the drying rack, and it was probably only my guilt, but I could swear that she knew more than she was letting on.

At work, I managed to organize the entire gay section and the straight gonzo section. I was dusting off the dildos when Randy came in. It was toward the end of the night, and when he saw all the work I'd done, he looked at me like I was nuts. He fished around for the source of my mania, but I wasn't ready to let on, not yet.

On the walk home, I tried to recall the panic I'd felt earlier in my sister's old bedroom. I tried to bring it back because it seemed like the correct way to feel, but I couldn't. Guilt just pinged through my body like a ball bearing, knocking against my heart, my gut, my head, but it wouldn't stick.

The fact was that I was having sex with Joey because I *wanted* to have sex with him. Because a part of me felt like I *deserved* to. Not just because she'd done it to me, with Nick, though that was my go-to justification. There was a deeper level to it. My mom and sister loved me, but only as a loveable fuckup, a puppy who shits on the carpet—it drives you crazy, but cleaning it up gives you a purpose in life. I'd graduated college, but even my choice of major had come down to what I thought they would want. I didn't want to get judged for being an art major. I'd fallen into their trap. Joey was my rebellion. Not to mention my sexual outlet.

So, it was with these feelings that I came home and found them curled up together on the couch. *My couch.*

I made myself something to eat, not so much because I was hungry, but because I didn't want to be around them. Joey, with his arms around Trisha, looked for all the world like her loving partner and nothing like the hornball who'd fucked me bareback that morning.

I listened to them murmur playfully as I ate, Joey's voice low and teasing, and then her voice, high and girlish. "Joey! Stop it!" *Giggle, giggle.*

It made me want to puke or blow something up, but I was done eating, and there wasn't anything to do in that house but sit with them. Joey was lying against the arm of the couch, Trisha spooned in against him, her hand on his casually spread thigh, his cock pressed against her back, presumably soft, but who knew? Joey played with her hair, twirling it in his fingers. Trisha wore a baby doll T-shirt with little straps that went over her shoulders, her breasts falling away from one another. She looked relaxed. They had to have just fucked.

They've probably been fucking all evening. Joey eating her pussy, her ass. Trisha sucking his cock. Both of them coming at the same time, being as loud as they want and grateful that I'm not around so that they can fuck as long as they want. Then lying there in each other's arms, professing their undying love.

"How was work?" Trisha said.

I shrugged.

"I go in late tomorrow," she said to nobody in particular.

"You didn't go in today?" I said, forcing myself to look at Joey. It was uncomfortable talking to both of them at the same time.

"They called me off. Gas leak in the building."

They went back to talking to each other, and I tried to watch TV, but it was an episode of *Law & Order: SVU* that I'd seen twice already this summer.

"I loved that picture you texted me," she said. Tracing a finger around his chin.

"Yeah?" Joey said. Cupping her butt in his hand.

"I wanna come see it. You've never taken me to the shop before." I assumed she was talking about the bookshelf Joey was building for her.

"I'll take you," he said.

"If you made some more stuff, we could sell it. Online...or we could get a table at the flea market on the highway."

"Yeah, that's a good idea," he said.

"I'm full of good ideas."

"You are, baby, you are." Kissed her. Started shallow, then went deeper and *I'm fucking sitting right there*.

I stood up. I only realized I'd made an exasperated sound when they both turned to me. Trisha looked surprised. It was Joey's look that gave me pause.

"Where are you going?" she said.

"Just a walk," I said. I'd already turned away. I couldn't stand it, that look. He was amused.

13

I resolved to stay away from him. It wasn't the first or last time I told myself that. It was a temporary relief from the guilt. I could pretend like I was taking the high road because I wasn't having sex with him anymore. I'd made a mistake, and I'd corrected it.

That was how I felt that morning when I sat with Trisha for breakfast. She made pancakes, with fresh blueberries.

"Joey still asleep?" I said.

"Yeah. I didn't want to wake him up. We were up pretty late last night."

I ignored this.

She asked, "How's the job?"

"We found somebody's teeth in the back the other day."

Trisha nearly spit out a mouthful of pancakes.

"I swear to God," I said, laughing. "They were sitting on top of one of the dividers between the booths. He came back an hour later to pick them up. I guess he just...got caught up in what he was doing."

"I'm so sorry," she said. "At least it seems amusing. Have you seen anybody we know?" she said, looking over the table at me.

I shook my head.

"Do any cute guys ever come in?"

"What, like, boyfriend material?" I said.

Trisha shrugged. "It'd be nice if it was a way to meet people.

I can't imagine that's easy to do in this town."

"It's all married men. I'm not interested," I said, the irony of my words a million times thicker than the syrup on my pancakes.

"Well, you're getting out of here anyway, right?"

"Right," I said.

"When is that happening?"

"End of the summer," I said, not looking at her.

"So, you'll be here until then?"

"I don't know. I guess so." I just wanted her to shut up. I didn't know and I couldn't think of how and it was driving me crazy.

◆

My resolve dissolved in as much time as it took for her to pull out of the driveway. Something about the silence of that house was enough to turn me on. Nobody was around, not for miles. You could do whatever you wanted and nobody would know.

It wasn't five minutes after she drove off that I heard the creak of the attic stairs.

Whump, whump, whump. Our code. My asshole dilated.

I could run. Put on clothes and shoes and just leave, take Mom's car and drive to New York or, fuck it, drive to California, then get a flight to Australia or Easter Island, for fuck's sake. Get as far away as I can, make a new life between me and this guy and my family that I've destroyed, am destroying.

But nobody knew. Not yet and maybe not ever. And that was what made it so exciting, that it was just between us, just *for* us. Damned if that didn't make my dick throb. I got up from the couch and opened the bedroom door. The faint scent of her aromatherapy thing, the ruffled sheets, the scarlet red light that came through the curtains. It was cloudy, threatening rain— weather that made you want to stay inside.

The door to the attic was closed, which was strange. *Did I imagine hearing him?* I thought. Just before I opened it, though, I noticed that their closet was open, just a crack. I looked inside as I passed it, and in the inky black, I *saw* someone, standing in the closet, staring at me.

She stayed to catch me.

No. Just her coat, hanging on the inside of the door. I'd imagined a large, shiny button on the lapel for an eye—a dead eye, like the one I'd seen in my nightmare.

I climbed the stairs. There wasn't any sound of porn this time, just the creak of each stair as I stepped up, then the sound of the fan in the window.

Joey was on the couch, but not like he'd been the last time, his cock in his hand, smiling. He was on all fours, his spread- wide ass pointed toward me, firm, round, and gorgeous. His hair-rimmed asshole flexed and released as he stroked the hard cock that jutted from underneath him, like the very act of exposing his hole was making him want to come. He arched his back as he heard me get closer.

"Like that?" he said, his voice breathy. He let go of his cock and it barely moved, diamond hard. I caressed his smooth lower back. He exhaled.

"Yeah," I said. The springs in the couch gave up muffled groans as I knelt in between Joey's feet. I felt his hairy calves, his thighs, stopping just before his ass. The smell of his ass—clean, but carnal.

"What do you want me to do?" I asked.

"Everything," he said, stroking himself, his face half-buried in the couch pillow.

"Does she ever play with your ass?"

"Never."

I licked up his legs, soft skin covered in hair, up his thighs, stopped just short of his ass cheeks. Then moved to his lower back, where his hair was downy and blonde and felt like peach fuzz on my tongue. I stopped just short of his crack. His ass and thighs got goosebumpy, and his breath was short and shallow. I kept doing that, licking all around his ass, but never inside, jumping around so he never knew where I was going to go next.

I was as hard as he was, but still in my shorts, my cock leaking through the front. I licked right up to the rim of his hole, paused, and finally wormed it inside. He went crazy, moaned like a scream.

"Oh fuck. Lick my ass."

I lapped against his hole, feeling it loosen and tighten again. I pierced it inside, past the tight muscle.

"I love it. I thought about it all last night."

"While you were fucking her?"

"That's how I came," he said.

I reached down and stroked his cock for him as I licked, getting my tongue in deeper, squeezing his ass cheek with my other hand.

"Goddamn, you're good at that," he said.

I touched the tip of my index finger to his asshole.

"Yes," he said. "Oh, fuck yes."

I pressed my finger hard enough so that it wasn't quite inside but was close. Then I got it wet and I pressed in again. He pushed back to meet it and the tip popped inside. I felt his hole instantly tighten. He was breathing, trying to relax, and finally, his hole loosened again and I pushed more inside. He was so tight, but he wanted it, and he pushed back to meet my finger, to get the whole thing sunk in him. Then it was inside to the second knuckle, so I pulled it back out and pushed it back in, and he moved his ass with me. He was fucking himself on my finger, his pink hole swallowing it up again and again. His cock was still hard.

"Dude, you have no idea how good that feels," he said.

"It might feel better with lube."

"Go get it from the bathroom."

I ran downstairs, noticed the quiet of the living room and kitchen, the way the fridge ticked softly as if marking the time.

When I got back upstairs, Joey was standing there, still naked, his hard cock jutting out in front of him. He was putting a record on his stereo—Led Zeppelin. He came to me and we made out. I grabbed hold of his butt, pressing my finger into his hole as we kissed. Joey's tongue went deeper into my mouth.

"I didn't know you liked your ass played with this much," I said.

"I told you that vibrator downstairs wasn't just for her."

"Does she know you like to use it?"

"Sort of. Anyway, she never really uses it." He got back on the couch, this time perpendicular to it so that his ass was

125

sticking out.

I lubed up my finger and slid it back in.

"Get another one in there," he instructed, so I did, and his cock never went down. "Now your cock."

"Are you sure?"

"Yeah, man. I want you to fuck me. Fuck, I want it so bad."

I took off my shorts, lubed up my cock. I have to say, I never fantasized about this. I always imagined him fucking me, sucking his cock, him sucking my cock. This was different. He was giving himself to me, and it was turning me on like crazy.

I brought my cock to his hole and he backed up onto it. Slowly, first the head, then a pause. Then he took the rest, me pushing up as he slid back until I was entirely inside of him. He was so hot and tight. He took it easily.

I held onto his creamy ass cheeks as I pulled back, till my bare cock was almost all the way out of him, then I shoved it back in. I'd never fucked anybody without a condom before—even my ex, Eric, had insisted on using one—and it wasn't so much the feeling of skin on skin (though that was intense) as it was doing it without preparation, without thought. Just fucking the way fucking was meant to be done.

"Oh, man," Joey said as I shoved it back in. "I love your cock in me."

"Yeah?"

"Yeah, man. Fuck me. Fuck my ass."

That basically did it. I got a few more shoves of my cock in him, but hearing him say that made me lose it.

"I'm coming," I said.

"Do it, brother. Come in my ass. Deep as you can. Fuck, I

wanna feel it shooting in me."

I couldn't say anything else as I shoved it in him to the hilt and let it loose, one forceful jet of sperm shooting into him followed by another and another.

I came off him and we sat next to each other on the couch. His cock was still hard. I apologized for getting off too soon.

"It's cool," he said. "You can fuck me again in a little bit."

So, we did, and this time, he came before I did, feeding me the come he'd shot onto his stomach as I pumped a second load into his ass.

We lay there on the attic rug, my head resting on his arm, sweaty and spent. Our sides were touching, one of my feet rested over his. I felt tender, tethered to him, like a soft rope was wrapped around my heart.

I'd felt like this with Eric.

I didn't have any sex my first year of college. In fact, I didn't even make many friends. But I moved to a different dorm my second year, and as soon as I saw Eric, I was attracted to him. He was shorter than me, but he carried himself with confidence. He was thicker, too, with a plump little butt and a dark beard. I figured he was straight until after we'd been living together a few weeks, and I got the courage to tell him I was gay.

"That's cool," he said. "I mostly date dudes, too." Like he couldn't be bothered to label himself.

I got somewhat obsessed with him as the year went on, this

sexy hippie who played Beatles songs on an acoustic guitar and was majoring in environmental science. He'd wear loose pants and nothing else around our room, and I wanted to get in them, but I felt confused about the whole situation. It seemed like, since we both "dated dudes," we should just be able to jump into bed with each other. The fact was, even though I'd come out over a year ago, I still hadn't spent much time around gay people.

Then one night I heard Eric jacking off in bed. I could see him in the moonlight, lying on his back, pumping his fat cock in his hand. I got hard and started doing it, too, then his eyes caught mine and he smiled at me. He nodded for me to come over to him, so I lay beside him in his bed and jacked off with him.

When we got close to coming, Eric turned to me. His face was close, his breath spicy. "Trade hands?" he said.

So we did, and came like that. Buckets.

After that, we kept doing it. Mostly at night. Then we started doing more, which became him fucking me almost every night for two weeks. I'd rim him for hours, his hole opening up around my tongue, before he flipped onto his back and had me ride his cock. I'd ride it gladly because it opened me up and made me come like crazy.

But that was when I started getting that tender feeling. We'd fall asleep after we came in his bed and snuggle up. He'd hold me or I'd hold him, and for those two weeks, it was like that.

Then the sex got more infrequent, but even less frequent was the tenderness. He'd roll over in bed after it was over, and sometimes I'd feel alone, even with him right beside me. The next year, he moved into an apartment. We kept hanging out, but it became more of a friendship. Which was fine, but in a way, it was worse than if we'd "broken up" officially. We'd never defined the relationship, so it was like I couldn't even mourn it being gone.

Lying with Joey, thinking of Eric, I suddenly wanted to cry. But I hid it. Then the shame of it all cascaded down and I felt paralyzed terror. I stared at the ceiling, and even though our bodies were close, it felt like we were on different ends of the planet.

"I like that we both dig getting fucked," Joey said. We were on the back porch, eating bowls of cereal.

"Me, too," I said. "You really never did it before?"

"No," he said. "I mean, I always kinda wondered. But I never thought I'd get off on it like I did." The birds chirped.

"Is it weird, fucking both of us?" I said.

Joey kept chewing. "Haven't really thought about it," he said. "It's easier with you. I know that."

"We really should be using condoms."

"Why?"

"I don't know. What if one of us gives the other a disease?" *And then gives it to my sister*?

Joey put down his spoon. He looked genuinely startled. "Do you have anything?"

"Not that I know of."

"Okay. Good." He took another bite.

"But what if I, like, go to the city and have sex with somebody and bring something back?"

"Are you going to?"

"Probably not," I said. I had no intention of going anywhere. That was the point and maybe the problem.

"You don't need to," Joey said, putting his bowl on the cement patio. He slid his hand up my leg. "I'm all you need."

We left our bowls there and went back to the attic, where I fucked him for the third time that morning.

14

My days took on a familiar routine: wake up and hang out with Trisha. Atone in my mind, self-flagellate. Watch her leave, listen to Joey climb the attic steps, feel guilt drain away, and lust rush in like water through a blown-up dam. Then the call: *whump, whump, whump*. I never resisted it.

One Saturday, Trisha drove me to work on her way to Mom's. We were going through town and on the corner was this guy. It was a hot day, and he was wearing just a pair of tiny red shorts that clung to his body like Saran Wrap, his thighs bulging obscenely. In fact, his whole body was built insanely huge, and he was tanned to within an inch of his life.

"Holy shit, is that Mike Dhalgren?" I said.

"It *is*," Trisha said. "He looks so *gay*!"

He really did. His blonde hair was frosted at the tips and gelled in precise spikes. He had a tribal design tattooed across his bicep. I mean, he was hot. But he also looked a little ridiculous.

The thing was, even though I hadn't been out in high school, Mike Dhalgren had made my life hell during freshman year, shoving me surreptitiously in the hall, sneering, "Fag," under his breath. He'd known I was gay practically before I had.

"I don't think I ever told you this," Trisha said, turning off Main Street. "We had calculus together. He would always say things about you...like, he'd flirt with me in this obnoxious way, always commenting on what I was wearing. But then he'd ask about you. If you were gay."

"What would you say?"

"I'd just ignore him. I mean, nobody really took him seriously. He was such a shit. But then one day, we were in the hall, and he was like, 'I saw your brother getting railed under the bleachers after the game on Friday by a bunch of black guys.'"

"I guess I'm not that surprised."

"Yeah. Well, I was sick of him. He was saying all this racist shit, too. So I punched him in the face."

"*What*?" I said. Trisha looked at me. She was proud, I could tell. I was a little shocked. I had no idea that she'd ever gone to bat for me. But I guess, at the time, I might have been even more embarrassed to talk to her about the fact that I was getting pegged as gay. "What happened?"

"I got detention. Remember when I got detention?"

"I do." My sister was such a goody two-shoes that she *never* got in trouble, so that time had stuck out.

"That was why."

"That's fucking awesome."

"Well...," she said, shrugging as she flipped her turn signal. "That was my angry period. I got in that fight with Christina around the same time. But punching Mike Dhalgren was pretty great. The look on his face. And you know what? He never bugged me after that."

"I bet he laid off of me around the same time. Thanks."

Trisha shrugged. "I was pretty much thinking of myself, but you're welcome."

132

"Here's the thing, though, Trish: I really *was* getting fucked by a bunch of black guys under the bleachers." Trisha was taking a drink of her coffee when I said this. She spit it all over the steering wheel.

I liked that I could joke with her still. But those moments came back to me, usually just after I'd come with Joey, his load in me or my load in him, the two of us lying on the floor of that attic. I'd think of Trisha and what she would think of me if she really knew who I was.

But then I'd do it all over again. Connect with her, connect with him. Up in the attic, Joey and I doing every depraved, porny thing we could think of with each other, usually talking about it in the context of *her*, of what he wasn't doing with her, what he'd only do with me.

Trisha was my sister. Joey was my come brother.

◆

A text from my boss: *The phantom shitter strikes again.*

I was hanging around the house with the two of them, a situation I was increasingly trying to avoid. The anxiety of it created a sort of schizophrenia. So, when Randy's second text came through—*I need to get high*—I texted him Trisha's address and he came to pick me up.

He pulled up in front of the driveway and I went down to meet him, a joint in my pocket. He tousled my hair as I got in the car. Randy knew I liked to get high and he'd hinted that he hadn't done it in a while, but so far, he'd never asked to partake. I had a good feeling as we cruised down Falling Run

Road in the waning evening sunlight.

"I worked all fucking night. From five yesterday to six this morning," he said.

"What happened to Elton?" I said. Elton was the night guy, usually pretty dependable.

"Called off. I can't really be mad at the guy because he's been working the night shift since time immemorial. But still. I'm too old for this shit. Literally."

"Where was it?" I said, watching Randy deftly maneuver his car along the bends and dips of Falling Run. It occurred to me that he was of this town as much as I was, even more so. There was something comforting about that.

"Same spot. Same...consistency even. I shit you not. Anyway, I got four hours of sleep and I want to get stoned."

"I got you covered," I said, pulling out the joint.

"Not yet," Randy said. "I know a good place we can pull off. At least if I can find it."

We drove about half a mile down Falling Run and turned off onto a dirt road. Randy's car bounced around on the rough road, and we stopped in a large meadow. We got out and leaned our butts against the hood of the car. I sparked the joint and handed it to him.

"Man, I haven't been out here in years," he said, taking a drag and handing it back to me.

"It's beautiful," I said. The meadow glowed in the late afternoon sun, bugs dancing on top of it.

"This used to be the spot, back in the day. Take a blanket, haul out a keg, stay out all night. Seems like nobody uses it anymore."

"People went out to Derry Lane when I was in high school," I said.

"We used to go out there, too." The crickets were chirping; the whole meadow sounded alive. "How's your summer going?" Randy said, holding in another hit.

"Oh, you know. I'm back in my hometown. I'm working at a porn store. I'm living with my sister and her boyfriend. And, uh, I'm fucking her boyfriend."

"What?"

"My sister's boyfriend. We've been fucking for the past couple weeks."

"Oh my god. Tell me everything."

So I did, every last detail. I could tell he found it pretty titillating, but then I did, too. Still, after I was done, he told me something surprising.

"My late partner, Dominic, he was once engaged to my sister," he said.

"You're kidding me."

"Nope. I mean, this was ages ago. In the seventies. Sometimes I even forget that it happened like that, but it did. That's how we met. And we fell in love pretty quick."

"What happened? With your sister, I mean?"

"Well, she hated me. For a long time. Truth be told, I think it took about a decade before we were talking to each other again. But, you know, I might have saved her a lot of grief down the road. Dom was gay."

"I don't think Joey's gay."

"Really? Interesting."

"Yeah. I think he likes having sex with both of us."

135

"And how do you feel about him?"

"I guess I just like having sex with him, too."

Randy nodded. The joint was done. "Sounds perfect."

"But what if she finds out?"

"Are you planning to tell her?" he said.

"No...no, I don't think so."

Randy shrugged. "Just keep it a secret."

Funny how he could just shrug off the emotional apocalypse I assumed was coming. But maybe it could just be a thing, a fling. Maybe he and my sister would break up eventually. He'd drift away, and I'd be off in New York. I could pretend it never happened.

"Believe me," Randy said, "I never wanted Becky to find out. But Dom felt he had to tell her, and then he left her. For me."

"Were you mad at him for telling her?"

"It's hard to remember. I don't think I was. He was just doing what he had to do. Plus, we were really in love."

"We're definitely not," I said.

"Doesn't make any difference. This is between him and you, for one thing. You didn't make any type of commitment to your sister. He's the one cheating."

"Technically."

"Sure, technically. The other thing is, he's still giving it to her. Are you guys playing it safe?"

"Uh...no."

"Sheesh. Okay. Well. You probably should use rubbers. I mean, everyone *should*. But then you're not really screwing around."

"Yeah, and I was just tested in March."

"Good. Get tested again soon."

"I will. It's just that I'm constantly beating myself up about it."

"Raised Catholic?" he said.

"How did you know?" We'd gone to church every Sunday when my Dad was alive. It was the one regular family thing we did. After church, we'd eat and then he'd go straight down to the basement.

"Lucky guess," Randy said. "Plus, it takes one to know one. Do you have anything to take your mind off it? Don't you draw?"

"I haven't drawn anything since I got back into town. That's a whole other thing. I'm supposed to be saving money to move to New York to make art, and I can't even make art here in Groom."

"Do something easy and stupid. Something that doesn't have your whole future tied up in it."

"I guess I could do that."

"And as far as the rest is concerned, just enjoy it. Don't get caught. And tell me *everything*."

15

Randy dropped me off and I wandered around for a couple hours until I sensed that they would be in bed and I wouldn't have to witness them canoodling on the couch. I wound up on the edge of town in a new housing development, half of it under construction with yellow backhoes in the backyards. I walked along the fresh white sidewalk until I found a bucket of sidewalk chalk someone had left at the edge of a yard. I thought about Randy's suggestion, and the next thing I knew, I was crouching over the sidewalk, drawing. I made a sunset. It was something.

When I eventually got back, it was late and they were asleep. I felt so horny that I decided to do something crazy. I took a shower, cleaned my hole. Then I slipped on my shorts and shoes and went outside. I crept around the back of the house where there was an old wooden ladder leaning against it. I propped it against the house and climbed up to the roof. Then I hopped over the eaves to the front, to the attic window.

I lifted the screen and carefully took hold of the box fan, which I set on the floor. Then I crept inside.

My head was swimming. What the fuck was I doing? But then I did it. *Whump, whump, whump.* Just the heel of my foot, just enough so that maybe it could have been mistaken for something else.

I heard the door open. I got an explanation in place, just in case: *I left my weed up here and had to sneak up to get it.*

138

Somebody started up the steps. I stayed back against the window. The footsteps stopped. Whoever it was shut the door behind themselves, and then I knew it was him. My cock started getting hard.

In the moonlight I could see him, wearing just a pair of boxer briefs, his cock tented out in the front of them.

"I hope I didn't scare you," I whispered. "I figured we could go down to your car."

"Why?" he said, coming toward me. He grabbed my cock through my shorts. "She's not gonna wake up." My sister does sleep like the dead, and I'd be lying if I said I hadn't been counting on that.

He kissed me, his tongue going into my mouth. I took his hand and put it around my body, into the back of my shorts, and with my other hand, I reached inside his underwear and wrapped my fist around his hard-on. Joey got the message. His fingers went for my hole, which I'd already lubed up in the bathroom. He slipped the tip of one finger inside and I moaned into his mouth, real soft and quiet.

"I want to get fucked so bad, Joey," I said.

"I can tell." He spun me around and pushed me against the wall, shoved my shorts down over my ass. He took hold of my ass cheeks and positioned his cock to my hole, letting it ride against it as he shifted his hips forward. "Feel how hard I am for you?" he said. He licked and kissed the back of my neck.

"Please fuck me."

He lined his cock up with my hole and pushed. The head popped inside and he kept going, inch after inch sliding in me just like I needed. I pushed back against him to take more.

139

Finally, he was in me to the hilt. He ran his hand up my torso, feeling my smooth tight body.

"I just fucked her," he said.

"In her pussy?"

"Yeah. She won't let me fuck her ass. It's so much better in the ass," he said, pulling out and pushing back in. "Tighter. And no rubber."

"I want your come in me. I want to leave it in me all night."

He pumped faster, smooth, fluid, dreamy motions. My body moving with his, taking him into me.

"Yeah," he said in my ear, so soft, the breeze from the window going over my naked body. "Then it'll be all lubed up for me to fuck you again, in the morning after she leaves."

"Yes. I want that."

His arms made a tight band around my chest as he shoved himself into me, faster and faster. "Gonna come," he whispered, then shoved it in me deep and held it there, letting his nuts unload into me, filling me up.

I pulled up my pajama pants, and he wiped his cock clean with a dishtowel he pulled from a box. He threw it on the floor and put his underwear back on. "Guess you'll have to climb down the roof again."

"Yeah," I said. He kissed me. He crept back down the stairs. I went back out into the quiet night, and everything was just as it had been.

"I had a dream," Trisha said that morning. I was eating a bowl

140

of cereal at the table, even though I wasn't hungry and the cereal was that fiber crap that looks like rat turds. Plus, I was out of two-percent milk, so I was using Trisha's soy milk that tasted like rancid watermelon juice. Breakfast as atonement.

"About the attic," she continued, and my whole body seized up. Trisha was boiling eggs on the stove, stirring them, staring out the window at the cracking dawn. She was still in her sleepwear, a baby tee and a pair of tight shorts. She looked sexy. She looked like the type of girl who shouldn't have a boyfriend sneaking into the attic at night to fuck her brother.

"There were owls up there—like, weird owls. Their faces were too big for their bodies. Almost human faces, but with owl eyes. They were in the corners of the attic up there and it wasn't day or night … it was half-night, you know? But I could hear them. I went up to investigate. I could see them in the dark with these wide, bulging eyes." She stirred the eggs in the sauce pan like a witch at a cauldron. "That's it. I went upstairs and opened the window, but I couldn't get them to fly out."

I didn't say anything. *She heard us and she saw us, but she doesn't know it yet, only her subconscious does, and it's only a matter of time before the truth surfaces, truth like wisdom, like a wise owl....*

She flicked off the flame on the gas stove and spooned the eggs out into a plastic container. "Anyway, dreams are stupid. Did I tell you I started reading Dad's book again?"

"Really?"

"Yeah. It's weird how sexual it is. Even more so because it never exactly gets explicit. But the Martians are like these sex gods. The Martians with their edible genitals."

"I remember that. They can regenerate them."

141

"So weird," Trish continued. "The under-earth world is all fleshy, too. Uric plants and flowers, and phallic trees and buildings, and everyone's naked. It's more poetic than I remember. It seemed pornographic to me—back then, I mean. He was still alive when I read it, but that was right around the time when things changed between us. Before I hit puberty, we were pretty close."

"Close? You and Dad?"

"Yeah," she said. "We used to go hiking up in the hills above Deep Hollow. I guess you were too young for that. We saw rattlesnakes."

"He never did anything like that with me."

Trisha shrugged. "He used to be more present." She was trying to soften the blow, but it bothered me that she'd gotten more of him than I had. Dad had always seemed sort of afraid around me, and even though he died before I hit puberty, I remember thinking he seemed confused by me for sexual reasons, like he could tell I was gay even before I could.

Sometimes I thought he died because of me, that it was my fault.

"Yeah. After I got tits, he stopped wanting to spend time with me. It hurt. It still does. But then he never spent a lot of time with either of us, I guess."

"Right," I said. Even so, I felt like I'd got the worst of him. My mom got to fall in love with him, my sister got to go on adventures with him, I got some genetics and this perverse drive to be an artist, and that was about it.

Trisha lit up a cigarette. She was pretty open about smoking lately.

142

"Mom's driving me crazy. I have to take her shopping to get a dress for Dustin's wedding," I said.

Trisha took a drag, blew it out, shrugged.

"Tell me," I said. "Why aren't you doing that?"

"She just wants somebody to ride with her. You'll have to go into the store, but it's not like she's gonna make you into her personal stylist," she said.

"It just feels like something that should be your job," I said.

"Please keep in mind that Mom has *been* my job for the last four years while you were getting your degree."

"So, now it's been passed onto me?"

"For a fucking *summer*. Until you go to *New York City*. You are still doing that, right?"

I swallowed my words and fumed silently, but my anger and emotions could swing wildly depending on how I looked at the situation.

I'm going to be fucking your boyfriend in a few minutes. Me in him and him in me, the two of us together, making out, bodies all over each other where yours just was, except it's different with me, raw and rough, and we come in each other....

I watched TV while she got ready for work and she left the house without saying anything to me.

He's probably asleep, naked, with morning wood. I could just climb atop him and ride, ride, ride, right there in her bed....

I heard Trish pull out and I went to the bedroom door. I knocked lightly, but didn't get an answer. I turned the knob and looked inside. Joey was asleep on his stomach.

"Joey," I whispered. I walked in. I could smell my sister, a whiff of something flowery that I associated with her. I went up

143

to the bed, stood next to it.

I'll just touch him some and see if he responds, and then we can go up into the attic. We don't have to do it here. We shouldn't do it here, in my sister's bed ... bad karma, bad energy, just bad....

I leaned over Joey and felt his leg, the smooth skin of it, his leg hair copious, but downy, sparser on the thick meat of his thigh. The sheet covered him mid-thigh, revealing the part just below his ass, the cleft dark, but with a sprig of hair, and the domed mound that led to his ball sack.

He stirred, moved his face against the pillow. I kept my hand on his thigh, unsure if he was aware of my presence, which was exciting. I felt like I could touch him wherever I wanted. He shifted as if burrowing himself deeper into the mattress. Once he settled, I set my hand on the firm muscle of his ass. I palmed it, cupped its round curve. I leaned down and smelled. My nose made contact with his ass by accident.

"Mm," Joey moaned, in his sleep or half-sleep. He backed his ass up, as if his cock was hardening and he was trying to set it flat against the mattress. I took it as my cue to run my fingers down his crack. I teased my fingertips toward the inside, but not quite all the way. Joey moaned again, backed up some more, still not quite awake, and I wondered if he knew it was me or if he thought it was her.

His perineum was swollen. He was definitely hard— throbbing, from the feel of it. I tickled it, my fingers darting up toward his asshole.

"Fuck yeah," he said, then turned to look at me. He smiled, a sexy sleepy grin. If there was a note of surprise there, I tried not to think about it. To him, maybe it didn't matter *who* it was.

144

"Morning," I said.

"Keep doing that," he said, shoving his face back into the pillow and pushing his butt against my hand. I could see his hole in the morning light, pink and inviting. The thought that I could just fuck that, that it was there for my own use, made my dick throb.

I ran my finger down his crack. When I touched his hole, he arched his back like a cat, pressing his ass up to meet my fingertip. "Fuck yeah," he said.

"Should we go upstairs?"

"Why?" It was what I'd been thinking, even if it wasn't what I wanted to hear him say. "She's not coming back. Even if she does, we'll hear her." Joey noticed my hesitation. "C'mon," he said. "Get in bed with me. Don't think about it."

It was easy not to think, with him. I slid in bed beside him. He smiled and reached for my head, pulling me close and opening his mouth to meet mine. We kissed. The smell of Trisha was stronger here, in her bed. The bed was soft and warm from his body. *Doing it in her bed and she has no idea....*

Joey was sleepy, and our bodies moved together and into one another with a slow ease. Joey slid off my shorts, took my cock into his hand, stroked it as he kissed me. When he flipped onto his stomach again, I knew that we were on the same page. My face went right to his butt. I sniffed around, and it was good and clean, so I licked the tip of his crack, real gentle. Joey was all about his ass, pushing it back into me, physically articulating his need for more. I teased him, running my tongue and hands all over his legs and ass for a good while before I finally made contact with his hole. I loved this inversion of

145

power, me servicing his ass, but with the goal of warming him up enough that I could slide my cock inside him.

I alternated between licking his hole and pulling his cock between his legs and sucking off the pre-come. I took as much as I could get into my mouth, but it was an awkward position for cock sucking. I'd slather my tongue up his shaft, lap his balls, then pierce my tongue into his hole. He moaned louder and longer each time. When I finally slid a finger in his ass, his cock got so hard. When I got a second finger inside, he got even harder.

He was so wet and loose that I didn't even need to use lube—just got some spit on my cock and slid it right in. I held him close, and he took my hands in his and pulled my arms around his torso. I fucked him like that, our bodies totally connected, my pumping pelvis slapping against his ass cheeks as I drilled him slow and steady.

This is the best sex I've ever had. We fucked and fucked and fucked. I would get close, then slow down and back off so that I could make it last longer. Joey was all about it, telling me how good it felt.

"Enjoy that ass, man. It's all yours." It was next-level sex, porn-movie sex. I got him on his back and stroked him as I fucked his ass, keeping us both on the verge. Finally, we came at the same time. His come shot over his head and all over the bed. The next few shots landed on his torso. The look on his face when he came was stunned gratitude. "I've never come like that in my life," he said.

The sheets were a mess and I was laying in them.

"We're gonna have to wash these sheets," I said.

"Sure," Joey said.

"But then what if she notices that we washed them? You never do laundry. She might notice that they're too clean."

"Dude, relax," he said. I did my best, slipping my shorts back on and heading back to my couch.

I felt like I couldn't take it anymore, this flux of moods—insane with lust one minute, and crushed with guilt the next. It felt worth it when we were doing it, felt like something I deserved. And I know this sounds crazy, but sometimes I felt gratitude toward my sister for Joey, for this opportunity, for unlocking this potential for sexuality that I'd never known could be this intense. I felt mature because of it, more like an adult than I ever had. This was what sex could really be like, I realized, absolutely intense and all-consuming.

But I knew that Trisha could be experiencing the same thing, that Joey was the invisible thread connecting us, facilitating the best sex of our lives.

I watched him gather up the sheets and take them into the basement. Sometimes he seemed evil to me, narcissistic, pathological. Other times he seemed like a tool my sister and I were both using, one we'd eventually discard.

He came back up, stood in the hall, smirking at me, naked. If he was evil, I was just as evil as he was because sometimes I *wanted* her to know, to shove it in her face that I could do this, could fuck her boyfriend, that I was her equal if not above her. Did I really hate her that much? Sometimes it felt justified. Hearing her bitch about Mom when I visited from college, implying that I was taking the easy route by leaving town, that I was coasting through college and coasting through life, whereas she'd assumed all the responsibility. I hated her for that, for blaming me when I was doing what any normal person would, what she could have easily done for herself if she'd been brave enough.

Besides, she did the same thing to you in high school. The constant source of consolation. I held onto it like a life preserver.

I put the clean sheets back on the bed when they were done. I cleaned the bathroom, too. The impossible illusion of clean, when who knew what microscopic things lurked underneath it all.

"Do you tell anybody about...?" I started to say "us," but stopped myself. "About what we do?"

"Nah," he said, staring at the TV. He'd put on some clothes.

"Not your friends or anything?"

"No. They're all homophobic. Why?" he said, turning to me.

"I don't know. It's not important. I just wondered." I watched as he took a sip of beer. "I mean, you're fucking a brother and a sister. It's kind of crazy. I thought you might... brag about it."

"I guess I never thought about it like that," he said and turned back to the TV.

16

Randy was behind the counter reading *Valley of the Dolls* when I came in.

"Good book?" I said.

"Christ, these poor girls. They never get what they want." He looked me over as I tossed my bag behind the counter and went to clock in. "You look relaxed," he said.

I shrugged.

He put down his book. "What I mean is, you look well fucked."

I took a deep breath.

"Sorry," Randy said. "Didn't mean to call you out."

"It's all good. Just my usual insanity. Fucking him like crazy and driving myself crazy with guilt when I'm *not* fucking him."

Randy nodded. A customer came in, young guy, wearing a blue shirt from an auto repair garage. His name tag said, "Smitty." Early twenties, lanky, strong jaw. Cute. He bought five tokens and went into the back.

"Oh, but I love a young one," Randy said, standing to watch him disappear into the darkness. He turned back to me. "I had really a good time last night, by the way."

"I did, too," I said. "After you dropped me off, I wound up drawing on the sidewalk with some chalk I found. It was... revitalizing."

"Nice!" Randy said.

"Eh. It was just a stupid chalk drawing."

"Hey. Whatever works."

The bell on the door rang again, and in walked a middle-aged guy I'd never seen before. His face was pockmarked, and he had frosted blond hair that was gelled in spikes. He walked up to the counter.

"Larry. Long time no see," Randy said.

"Sorry I haven't been around, baby," he said and kissed Randy on the cheek. He smelled like cologne. I liked this guy. He might have been the first femme gay guy I ever met. "Winter in Boca, then looking after Mom because my idiot brother ordered a girl from the Philippines. They ran off and got married. But!" he said, his rings cracking against the counter as he laid his hands on it. "I got her a nurse. *Someone* should have to get paid for putting up with the old crone." He gave me a sincere look. "I really do love my mother."

"I'm sure," I said.

"This is Nate," Randy said. "Nate, Larry."

"Larry the Fairy," he said, holding out his limp hand. I thought I was supposed to kiss it, but we ended up shaking. "Charmed, I'm sure."

"Ain't he a dish?" Randy said of me.

"I don't know where you find them," Larry said. "Five, please." I took his money and doled him out five paper tickets. He reached into his pocket and came out with a thick roll of the same tickets, held together by a rubber band.

"Wow. You've got a stockpile," I said.

"Well, I don't care much for cinema," he said as he undid the rubber band and folded in the five new tickets. "Real life is

150

so much more compelling."

"Larry can suck the chrome off a tailpipe," Randy said. "In fact, you won't believe what just walked in a few minutes ago."

"Oh yeah?"

"Straight from Vale Tech, from the looks of it." Vale Tech was the auto repair school by the river.

"Gotta go. Momma's hungry," Larry said and headed into the back.

A few minutes later, Randy went through the back as well and returned to report on Larry's progress. "On her knees and happy as a clam."

"Clam sauce for dinner, I guess," I said.

Randy left to run some errands. The strong-jawed boy walked out a little later, sheepish, holding the brim of his baseball cap like it was a freshness seal of masculinity that he didn't want to break. Larry came out behind him holding a travel-sized bottle of hand sanitizer. He squirted some into his palm and rubbed them together.

"What'd you guys do?" I said.

"We picked out china patterns. What do you think?"

"Was it big?" I said.

"Rude," Larry said. "I'm kidding." Larry shrugged. We watched baseball-cap boy drive away in his loud truck. "Nothing to write home about, but it hit the spot."

"Did you swallow?"

Larry rolled his eyes at me. "A lady never tells," he said. "Of *course,* I did."

Sometimes I'd be sitting at that counter, watching the bright, normal world outside the window and thinking of

151

what was going on in the depths of this innocuous little store on the side of the highway. Then what went on in stores like this all across the country. It was this whole hidden world that everyone just accepted, or maybe they didn't know about it.

Larry snapped the cap back on his hand sanitizer and slid it in his bag. "That was just an appetizer for me, though," he said, looking me up and down. "You got anything I could snack on?"

"I'm working," I said.

"Oh, please," Larry said. "You should see your boss when *he's* working."

Just then, Randy's truck pulled up to the store. We watched him get out, drop something on the sidewalk in front of the store, and get back in his truck. He honked as he pulled away.

"What was that about?" Larry said.

We went outside. Randy had dropped a bucket of sidewalk chalk there. I laughed.

"I don't get it," Larry said.

"He's encouraging my artistry," I said. I was touched.

"Figures," Larry said. "First cute faggot he's ever hired, and he wants him to spend his time *outside* of the store instead of in the back."

◆

On Saturday, I swallowed my pride and went shopping with my mom for wedding clothes. She was sitting in the living room when I got there, purse in her lap, all ready to go.

"I thought we could go to the mall in Indiana and then try the outlets in Mon Ridge."

"Jesus, Mom. That's, like, an hour away."

"Oh, what do you have to do today anyway?" I thought of Joey and Trisha home alone, and me negotiating my insane mental middle ground. No, I didn't have anything to do that day. "And don't you need to buy a suit?"

"How many times have I told you that I have one?" I said.

"But you don't know where it is."

"It's somewhere upstairs in a box. I know it's there. I'm not, like, imagining it."

"Well, you never know with you."

I took a deep breath. We hadn't even left the house.

The mall wasn't bad because we separated and did our own things. I went to some trendy store I'd never shopped in before and found a baby blue suit jacket that spoke to me. I figured I could make it work with what I already had. Mom caught up with me just as I was about to check out and bought it for me, which was nice of her.

"Don't you think it's a bit flashy?" she said on the ride to the outlets.

"That's the idea, Mom. I'm trying to get more attention than the bride."

"Oh, come on now...."

"I'm *kidding*. Fuck's sake, it's a blue jacket."

"Please don't swear."

"I'm sorry."

"You just never know how those people are going to react to things."

"*Those* people?"

"Mormons. You know there's not going to be any alcohol

153

at the wedding."

I went to say, "Oh fuck," but caught myself before it came out. A dry wedding had never occurred to me. I resolved to buy a flask. "How long has Dustin been with this girl? I don't think I've seen him since I was a sophomore."

"Well," Mom said, getting excited. "You know that she's *oriental*."

"I think Asian is the preferred term."

"Well, she's from China or Korea or wherever he went on his mission. Which was only a couple of years ago, but next thing you know, she's over here and they're planning a wedding. It just makes you wonder."

"Makes you wonder what? Sounds like they fell in love and she's moving here to be with him."

"Well, who *knows* what goes on where she's from?"

"Hard to say when we don't even know her nationality."

Before we left the mall, I popped a Marinol pill that I'd had stashed away, one Eric had given me before I left Pittsburgh. By the time we got to the outlets, I was feeling mellow and happy. I even helped her pick out a dress. I played up the role of the fabulous gay son, and she was into it, but mostly I was glad to get away from Groom for a bit.

Joey was on a different work schedule that week, which meant that I didn't see him much. I welcomed it. Waking up and spending the day alone in the house was a respite from all the crazed lust I'd been experiencing. I could forget about it

154

all for a while. But I did sneak into the attic on Tuesday night and have sex with him again. And during the day, sometimes I would pull his dirty jockey shorts out of the laundry and jack off to the smell.

One day I found a Frederick's of Hollywood catalog on the kitchen floor. It looked like it had fallen out of Trisha's purse. I brought it to her outside in the backyard with a smirk.

"Nice, Trish. I didn't even know they made this anymore."

"Where'd you get that?" she said, snatching it out of my hand.

"It was on the floor!"

She tossed it behind her chair. Joey winked at me.

"Mom said you guys got her a nice dress. Did you help her try it on?" she said.

"No, but I bought a dress for myself."

"Sure you did," she said, puffing a cigarette.

I sat across from them in the grass. "It's from Frederick's of Hollywood, so it'll probably get in around the same time as your crotchless panties."

Trisha gave me another angry look. Joey got up.

"You're an ass," she said once Joey went inside. "That catalog is for Joey anyway. Not that you'd understand what it's like to have a boyfriend and want to please him."

"Gross," I said.

Trisha shrugged.

"Anyway," I said, "I had a boyfriend in college, remember?"

"Whatever. He was your *roommate*, right?"

"That's how it started out."

"Sure. Sounds convenient."

155

You have no idea.

They'd been planning a Mexican dinner all week. Joey was going to make tacos. Trisha was obnoxious about it, talking up his tacos like they were manna. All part of her campaign to make him domestic, I guess.

By the time he got out of the shower, she was getting things started in the kitchen.

"Where's the cilantro?" she said. "I swear we had some left. Didn't we?" She turned to me. "Did you use it?"

"Nope."

Joey walked into the kitchen. He wore a pair of shorts and was drying his head off with the towel.

Trisha looked him up and down, seemed annoyed by his half-naked body. "I guess we'll have to get some," she said to him. "If we're going to make guacamole."

Joey swirled the towel over his head, draped it over his shoulder, nodded. "Yeah, definitely," he said.

"Okay," she said, hesitating. "I guess...I could just run down there and get it. If you want to get the chicken started?"

"Yeah, sure," he said. He glanced at me. It was just a glance, nothing more, but it made my dick twitch.

Trisha got her purse. It was the most awkward thing— she clearly didn't want to leave, but she'd walked into the responsibility and didn't know how to get out of it. When she kissed Joey goodbye, he pulled her head in close and kissed her deeply. He looked at me the whole time he was doing it.

As soon as she was out the door, he turned to me. His cock was starting to chub up in his shorts. He dropped the shorts and stepped out of them. I watched his cock get fatter and start

156

to bob as he walked toward me.

"I thought she was never gonna leave," he said, pulling me into him. He kissed me and I melted into it. Christ, it was so hot, the way he played us off of each other. He took my wrist and brought it behind him, pressing my hand into his crack. I felt his hole, which was all lubed up. My finger slid right in, and soon I had another finger in beside it.

"You lubed up in the shower?" I said.

"Yeah."

"How did you know she was going to leave?"

"'Cause I threw the cilantro in the trash earlier."

"Fuck, Joey."

I flipped him around and wrapped my arms around his torso. There were times when I felt like we were "making love," as lame as that sounds. Holding him from behind, my cock poking at his hole, my hands all over his chest and stomach, nuzzling my mouth against his neck—it all felt so close and intimate.

He braced himself against the kitchen counter and adjusted his hole until it sank right over my cock. That moment of going into him or him going into me, skin against skin, the tight conjoining of it, bodies physically connected by this tendril of pleasure—I lived for it. Joey's moans filled the house as I pumped my cock in and out of his ass.

"Fuck, I've needed this for days now," he said. "It's all I've been able to think about. Fuck me."

Him saying "fuck me" always did it for me, and he knew that. It was the surefire way to get me to come—this butch guy *wanting* it, demanding me to fuck him, the dominant and the submissive all topsy-turvy.

"I'm gonna come," I said.

"Jack me off."

I wrapped my hand around his cock and pumped. We managed to come at around the same time, me inside him and him all over the counter, his asshole spasming around my cock as he shot off.

I pulled up my shorts and Joey pulled up his. I got a paper towel and was going to clean his come off the counter. "Maybe we should put it in the tacos?" Joey said with a gleam in his eye. It was just a joke, but I almost believed he would do it. I wiped up the come, buried the towels into the bottom of the trash next to a bunch of perfectly good cilantro.

We sat on the front stoop. The sun cast long shadows over our shoulders. I lit up the remains of a joint I'd rolled yesterday.

"Sucks that I've been working this new schedule," he said.

"Yeah," I said. I wasn't sure if it sucked. It was taking some of the pressure and stress away, to not have to think about it. "At least you can still fuck Trisha."

"Eh, it's not the same." He picked at something on his big toe. I sensed he was going to continue and prepared myself to listen, feeling both fascination and trepidation. "We just fuck, mostly. She barely ever sucks my cock. I used to eat her out a lot, but she seems weird about that lately."

I wondered if he was making it sound bad on purpose. Truthfully, I couldn't tell how I wanted it to be for them, for her. I could imagine Trisha micromanaging every aspect of sex, telling a guy exactly how to eat her out, giving him a goddamn map of the territory before he even got down there. That was probably how she was with her old boyfriends. With Joey, I suspect it was different. She was the beautiful, slightly icy girl with a good job and upbringing, and Joey was the blue-collar rascal who'd fucked her properly for the first time.

And me. In some alternate reality, it was something that could have brought us together—the best fuck we'd ever had.

Joey sucked the roach down to the nub and tossed it into the yard. "Anything else you want to know?"

"No," I said.

"Don't worry about it," Joey said, which was a weird thing to say. "She can't fuck me. That's the thing. I can't even get her to finger my ass when she sucks me. My ass is for you only."

I started getting hard. He noticed and felt it with his hand. Trish was gonna be home any second.

"Same with your ass for me," he said and slid his hand into the back of my shorts. He pressed his finger to my hole and it popped inside. "Same with our come. Only for us. That's how it's different than it is with her. It's closer."

Really, it was further apart. There weren't clear emotional connections between us. Our attachment began with our cocks inside each other and ended with a fluid exchange.

He took my hand and brought it to the back of his shorts. I felt down his back, my finger passing between his cheeks to his lube-sticky hole. I pressed in, fingered him just like he was fingering me. He kissed me. "Me in you and you in me. Come brothers."

We heard a car come up the road. "That's probably her," I said and went to take my hand out of his shorts. In one quick move, Joey grabbed my wrist with his free hand and held it

159

there so that I couldn't take my finger out of his hole, just as Trisha's car appeared, coming down the winding road.

"She can't see yet," he said. He was right—the stoop wasn't immediately visible from the road or even from the bottom half of the driveway. "Don't take your finger out until I say."

Trisha's car turned up the driveway. I was panicking a little, but I went along with it. Joey shoved his finger into me deeper, stretching my hole. I did the same. I could feel my load in him, coating his insides, gliding the way for my finger. Trisha turned off the engine. I heard the click of her engaging the parking brake. From her perspective, she could only see our heads, the upper part of our torsos. Her brother and her boyfriend, bonding on the stoop.

She opened the door. "Hey," she said to Joey. She grabbed the groceries from the passenger side and got out of the car.

"Hey baby," Joey said, working his finger inside me. She slammed the door shut with her hip, started up the driveway. Without a moment to spare, Joey took his finger out of me and I did the same.

He stood up. His cock was tumescent. Did she notice it? I stayed seated because I was completely hard. My finger was slick with come. When Joey went to kiss her, she turned her head and let him peck her on the cheek. She held the cilantro in one hand, a box of peaches in the other.

"Is the chicken ready?" she said.

"Shit," Joey said. "I'll start it right now."

Trisha's face fell. She looked at me like I was the one to blame.

I sort of was.

160

17

Joey and I were on opposite schedules into that week, and my sexual energy began to get pent-up. Sometimes I projected this into a passionate hatred of Trisha. They were disgustingly all over each other in the mornings, lovey and melty. I'd put the pillow over my head, but could still hear them murmuring to each other like they were part of the same underwater world and I was the bottom feeder, waiting to suck the scum off the prettiest fish.

In the evenings, if they were still up, Joey would toss me little bones. Grabbing my cock when she wasn't in the room. Letting me peek at his. One morning, right after they had left and Trisha had started the car, he came back in the house, to the couch. I was lying on my stomach. He reached into my shorts and grabbed my ass.

"I need to fuck you," he said in my ear.

"Right now?"

"No," he said, like it was obvious. "Tonight. The attic. Or we'll get her out of the house somehow. I can't stand it, man." His hand worked against my ass, fingers pressing into my hole. I pushed back against him, half-asleep and horny. He took out his hand and got his finger wet, put it back into position and slid it in. "See?" he said, and popped open the button on his jeans. I looked. He wasn't wearing underwear. His hard cock popped out like the clown from a jack-in-the-box.

Outside, Trisha honked the horn.

He took my hand and wrapped it around his cock. "You know you want this in you."

"I do."

"I want it, too, man." He slid his finger out of my ass. He put it to my mouth and shoved it inside, and I licked it clean, tasting my ass on his finger. "Don't jack off today. Save it for me."

"Okay."

And so we did the attic thing again. Us up there in secrecy, Homos in the Attic, while Trisha slumbered below, oblivious.

He had us make a pact that we wouldn't wear underwear around the house, whether she was around or not. The weather was sweltering and we were always in shorts, so our cocks and asses were always available to each other. Once I groped him in the kitchen while Trisha vacuumed the bedroom, the open door of the fridge blocking her view as I stroked Joey's cock in his shorts to a full erection then bent down to kiss it and slide it deeply into my throat, just once, just 'cause we couldn't resist, or maybe because we needed to push the boundaries to keep ourselves interested.

Maybe that was why I started to really love my job around that time. I found myself looking forward to going in. Partly, it was to hang out with Randy. Sometimes we'd get high before work.

I made use of the sidewalk chalk. I did a pop-art hot dog mural, just sexual enough that not everybody would notice, a guy eating it with a crazed look in his eyes and spittle flying everywhere. Randy loved it.

"People keep talking to me about it. Which is great because,

163

the vast majority of the time, they barely make eye contact with me. It's amazing how something small like that can break people out of their normal mode," he said.

I did another one a few days later when the rain washed away the first. I decided to continue with the double entendres and depicted a train entering a tunnel, except I got really into it. I drew a late-afternoon sunset, the light from it casting shadows on everything. I did the hills surrounding the tracks, drew myself walking along them, joint in hand. A road into the hills above, a motorcyclist riding off alone and into the sunset. It was so fun.

Later that night, Lloyd came in, our steady regular, the guy who practically lived in the back. I often wondered about him. He looked to be in his late sixties, if not older. Rail-thin and wrinkled, he looked like he'd been left out in the sun too long. He wore thick amber-tinted glasses and a railroad cap, and I honestly didn't know what he did back there all day when he wasn't sucking cock. He'd never said a word to me, not even when he bought his tickets.

But that night he looked right at me. "What's with the chalk art?" he said, only real fast and Western-PA-accented, so it sounded like one open-voweled mush: *whaswhida chawkart?*

"I drew it," I said, taking the five from his hand and handing him his tickets.

"At's pretty good," he said and actually smiled at me. "Looks like summer."

I smiled. Summer had been what I was going for.

Then he actually held out his hand. "Lloyd," he said.

"Nate," I said, shaking it.

164

"Hey, have a good one." He went into the back.

After that night, he would always nod at me. Even when he ducked out of the booths. We ceased to be strangers. I liked that.

◆

A couple days before the wedding, I went to my mom's house to find my suit. She wasn't home, so I let myself in the back door and went upstairs to my old bedroom to go through my boxes. I sat on the floor and started unpacking the accumulated detritus from my college years.

The sunlight coming through my bedroom window was at a harsher slant, and it occurred to me that it was late July; summer was two-thirds over. Moreover, I had nothing prepared for a move to New York and was steadfastly avoiding the subject. I suppose I had more immediate things to worry about.

What the fuck was I going to do? I had this absurd vision of myself still living with Trish and Joey when I was forty, sleeping on their couch and trudging to the porn store. Then the awful prospect of Trisha kicking me out so that I had to live with my mother.

I didn't want any of that, but I had no idea where to start. The one saving grace was that I had about a thousand bucks saved up, both from the store and from the security deposit money I'd received from my last apartment in Pittsburgh.

Aside from that, I didn't know a soul in New York and felt pretty certain that a grand wouldn't get me shit. It all got conflated with the fact that I was spending my time covertly destroying my relationship with my sister.

I sat there, having a minor panic attack, until I heard my mom come home. I called down to let her know I was there, then searched frantically for the suit. I pulled it out just as she came upstairs.

"Oh, so you *did* have it," she said.

"I told you I did." Actually, I was relieved because I thought I'd given it to somebody.

"Hm," Mom said, looking at the floor. I followed her gaze: Dad's book was laying there, the copy I'd kept since his death, the only copy that had been around our house after his death.

"I hope it's okay that I took that," I said.

"Oh, sure."

"Do you ever reread it?"

"No," she said dismissively. "It's such an awfully strange book. I suppose I never really understood it. Martians who are girls and boys, all that goofy otherworldly stuff. It never meant that much to me."

"Yeah, but you still get his fan mail."

"I throw that away, too."

"I went up to his grave the other day," I said.

"I haven't been there in years. Years and years," she said.

I was on the back deck at Trisha's, smoking a joint, when she and Joey came home. She was carrying a shopping bag.

"We bought Joey a suit," she said.

166

"You mean, *you* bought it?" I said.

"What's it matter?" she said.

"It doesn't. Sorry," I said, hating how nasty I'd sounded.

"I'm making dinner," she said. "I need rent for August, by the way."

"Sure," I said.

"Hey," Joey said, coming through the back door as Trisha went back inside. His ever-present smirk. He took the joint from my hand and took a big hit.

"So, you're going to the wedding?" I said.

"Seems like it," he said. "Hope there's an open bar."

"Dude, it's a Mormon wedding."

"What's that mean?"

"No booze. No coffee, even."

"Fuck," he said. He let out his hit. "Have to bring a flask, I guess." He looked at the shopping bag Trisha had left on the concrete. Looked at me. "Guess I better try on this suit."

He took the bag inside. I understood what he was getting at when he opened the bedroom curtains, which looked right out onto the patio. I turned around. He'd closed the bedroom door. I could hear the whoosh of water from the faucet where Trish was working in the kitchen.

Let the show begin, I thought.

The bedroom was dark, but he was lit by the bright outdoor light filtering in. He set the bag on the bed. Caught my eye for just a moment, gave me a quick smile. I smiled back. My palms started to sweat. He stripped off his shirt, running his hands over his smooth, muscular body. Pants next, and his big old hard-on bounced as he took his jeans off each foot. He stood

167

next to the bed, right against the window, looking right at me as he stroked his cock. I watched him unpack the shopping bag, lay out pants, a jacket, a shirt wrapped in plastic, stroking himself between each item, one eye on the bedroom door.

He slid on the pants without putting on any underwear, then put on the rest. It was a good look, the suit fit him—he cleaned up well. He left the bedroom, and I heard Trisha cooing over him in the kitchen. Then he went back in the bedroom and the show resumed. Took off the shirt, undid the pants and let them slide down to his thighs. Then he got on the bed on all fours and spread his bare ass out for me. What if Trisha walked in? He winked his pink hole at me, got a finger wet in his mouth and pressed it to his hole, slid it inside.

I had my hand down my shorts the whole time, tweaking my half-hard dick. Joey took the finger out of his ass and stood up. He put his ear to the door. When he was satisfied that she was busy, he went to the dresser and took out the pink dildo. He sucked on it, getting it wet with his spit, watching me the whole time. Then he came close to the window, his ass about a foot below the sill, and slid the dildo into his ass.

"Wish it was your cock," he whispered. I got my hand wet with spit and started jacking off under my shorts. He brought his finger, the one that had been in his ass, and pressed it to the window screen, his skin bisecting into little cells, like a waffle. I put my nose up to it, took in the earthy smell of his ass on his finger as I watched that pink dildo spread him open.

I came right in my shorts. He heard me and a satisfied smile spread across his face. I watched him put the dildo back in the dresser (thought, *I hope he cleans it at some point*) and put his shorts back on, his cock going slowly down.

"Dinner's about ready!" Trisha called from the kitchen.

Whenever she made dinner, Trisha insisted that we eat at the table.

"Mom said you bought a gay jacket," she said, dumping parmesan onto her spaghetti.

"She really said that?"

"No, she just described it, and I figured it out."

"Well, it is. That's why I like it. I want those Mormons to know."

"We're taking flasks," she said.

"Me, too."

"Getting fucked up is the only way I'm going to get through this one. Between Mom and Aunt Miriam. Plus, I think Mom's bringing Donna."

"Like, as a date?" Joey said.

"Gross!" I said. "Oh my god, what if Mom was a lesbian?"

"She's not. C'mon," Trisha said. "Remember that UPS guy she had a crush on after Dad died?"

"He used to flirt with her," I said, remembering. Then Trisha said something really quiet. I had to ask her to repeat it.

"I caught them once," she said, looking at me with wild eyes.

"Oh my god."

"I was home early from school 'cause I was sick. They told me they called Mom, but they didn't. It was a mixup. I walked home, and when I got there, the UPS truck was parked out in front and they were ... doing it upstairs. I heard them. Oh, christ...."

"I can't believe you never told me this."

"I never told *anybody* this. Well, actually, I think I told Julie. She caught her parents screwing before, too."

Seemed that my Mom had secrets just like the rest of us.

18

We were picking up Mom on the way to our cousin's wedding, in Joey's car, Joey driving, Trisha in the front seat and me in the back.

Joey looked handsome. His mustache was trimmed down and his hair was freshly shorn. Trisha looked good, too, in a purple dress that set off her red hair. She took Joey's hand as we rounded a curve in the road. I looked at the come stains next to me in the back seat from the first time Joey and I fooled around. I picked at one with my finger and put it to my tongue, but it didn't taste like anything.

I was feeling fresh. I'd trimmed my hair, and the jacket looked good with the rest of my suit. I knew I was going to stand out in the crowd, but I didn't care. I was actually excited to see some of my cousins. I guess it made me realize how isolated I was, out there in the country with mostly my sister and her boyfriend.

"Might as well get started now," Trisha said as she pulled a silver flask out of her purse. She took a swig and handed it to Joey, who drank from it and handed it to me.

"Don't we have to pick up Donna?" I said.

"No, she and Mom had a fight," Trisha said, taking the flask back from me. As the alcohol went through me, I got this feeling, all of us looking so good, that maybe it could be like this if Trisha and Joey got married. Just close family, the three of us. With me still fucking Joey on the sly.

Mom was waiting on the porch when we pulled up.

"Goddammit, you didn't tell me she bought a purple suit," Trisha said to me. I stifled laughter—Mom's suit was the exact same shade as Trisha's dress. I'd never thought twice about it.

"It's good. Now everybody will know that you're mother and daughter," I said.

"Christ," she muttered. Then, "Hi, Mom!"

Mom walked up to the car. She looked at the car as if appraising it.

Trisha got out and held the door open for Mom.

"Joey's driving us?" she said.

"Yep," Trisha said. I braced myself.

"This car runs well? It'll get us there?"

I snickered. Joey smiled back at me.

"I guess we'll find out," Trisha said, sighing. "Did you want to sit in the front?"

"Sure," Mom said. Trisha settled beside me, right atop the come stains.

"Hello, Joey. Don't you look handsome?" Mom said.

"Thanks, Janet. You look lovely."

Mom beamed. She looked around the interior of the car. "What an interesting vehicle," she said.

"Don't worry, Mrs. A. It's in good shape. I just put on new brakes this winter." I thought the "Mrs. A" was a nice touch, if a bit sitcom-y.

"Stylish, isn't it?" Mom said, looking back at us. We nodded. Trish looked at me, rolled her eyes. Mom settled into her seat. "Boy, wait till Miriam sees us pull up."

My mom's sister Miriam had once been a constant presence

172

in our life, good friends with my Dad, always at our house when we were young. But shortly after my Dad's death, she and my mom had a falling out for reasons I never fully grasped. I missed the lady. She was skinnier than Mom, smoked like a chimney, and cussed like a sailor.

"Did you buy this car, Joey? With your own money?"

"Yes, ma'am," Joey said, which made me snort.

"That's a rude question," Trisha said.

"Oh, I'm not trying to be rude," Mom said, looking out the window. "I know you love this guy," she added, reaching over and grasping Joey's shoulder. Joey smiled. I cringed.

The wedding was outdoors. There was a white arch where the ceremony was going to be held, chairs in front of it, next to a big pavilion that would house the reception. We parked in a field, under a big tree. Mom and Trisha got out of the car, and Trisha helped Mom across the lawn. Joey and I lagged behind. I could smell his cologne. I wanted to take his hand. Sometimes I had to fight those urges.

"Good thing it's nice out," I said. There were rainbow-colored balloons tied to the corners of the pavilion, and enough of them that it looked like it could sail away. An in-ground pool was next to the pavilion. Some kids were swimming. I spotted some familiar relatives, including my older cousin Kevin, who I'd had a crush on in high school. He had some skinny, long-haired girl on his arm. His dad was there. He was hot, too. And there was my Aunt Miriam, looking right at us as Mom had predicted. She waved. I waved back.

Joey leaned into me, spoke into my ear. "Maybe later we can go skinny dipping," he said.

"That'd be nice," I said. Ahead of us, Trisha and Mom had stopped. Trisha was helping adjust the broach on Mom's suit. Mom kept looking up at Miriam and back down at Trisha, who was struggling to get it pinned. We stopped a few yards behind them and Joey lit up a cigarette.

"I'm horny," he said. "I came out last night and tried to wake you up."

"I don't remember," I said.

"You were sleeping pretty hard," he said. Then, whispering: "All I could think about was your tongue in my ass." Mom and Trisha started walking again. Mom had given up on the broach and was stuffing it in her purse. "I brought lube just in case."

"Where is it?" I said.

"My pocket," Joey said, sucking on his cigarette. "One of those little plastic things of it."

"We can't fuck here."

"We can go off into the woods," he said.

I started walking. The thought of having sex at this wedding had never crossed my mind, and now that it had, it bothered me that it turned me on. I'd been looking forward to spending some neutral time with the three of them, without any skeezy thoughts in my head.

"You want to?" he said.

I couldn't make that decision. I gave him an exasperated look and caught up with Mom and Trisha.

The wedding was cute. Dustin seemed happy. By nightfall, the reception was in full swing. I'd finished half of my flask, and it was clear that my family wasn't the only one sipping booze on the sly. Kevin, my sexy cousin, was sharing one with his girlfriend—we'd traded swigs earlier. And then Dustin, the groom, caught me drinking from mine and asked for some.

"Dude, I thought you were Mormon," I said.

"I am," he said, taking a drink and handing it back to me. "I'm also fucking *married*, so fuck it."

The bride came up to us. Her name was Esmerelda, she was from Portugal, and she was pretty and personable. I'd lumped Dustin in with the rest of his boring Mormon family for so long that I'd forgotten he was cool. His family—my Uncle Joe, his wife, who he'd converted to Mormonism for, and their three other boys, all older than Dustin and all married—sat at a round table, looking generally miserable. I tried to slip the flask back into my pocket before Esmerelda noticed, but she did anyway. Her eyes got wide and before I knew it, the three of us were ducking behind the arch and passing it around.

"This is a great wedding," I said.

"Thank you!" Esmerelda said in her thick accent. "This was all I wanted. Outdoors, under the stars." Dustin beamed.

The DJ switched songs—"Don't Stop 'Til You Get Enough." I looked back at the dancers. Trisha was there, cutting a rug. I'd never seen her look so unselfconscious. She put her hands above her head, red hair swinging with her dress.

She locked eyes with somebody. Joey. His tie was loosened,

the top two buttons of his shirt undone. I could see his ubiquitous wifebeater underneath. They danced toward one another. Joey wrapped his arms around the small of her back. His pelvis met Trisha's and they danced close, grinding a little. Her movements were liquid, effortless. Joey nuzzled into her neck. He put his hand on her ass and squeezed. Trisha threw her head back, laughing. She swung around and Joey pulled her back into him, his pelvis against her ass now.

"Nate," Dustin said. He held the flask to me. I'd been completely absorbed in watching them. "You gonna dance later?"

"I think so," I said.

"I want to dance now," Esmerelda said, and Dustin led her away. My mom came out onto the dance floor. People were cheering her on. She danced awkwardly, but committedly. It made me smile.

Joey took Mom by the hand. She seemed surprised, but went with it. Joey looked her in the eyes. He spun her around. Mom's face was lit up.

He couldn't dance with you if you went out there. He wouldn't.

"What you got in that flask?" Aunt Miriam had snuck up on me.

"What flask?" I said.

"Aw, c'mon. Don't yank my chain. I seen you drinking out of that all night."

"It's milk."

"Well, give me a swig. Doctor says my bones are getting brittle." I handed her the flask. She took a healthy gulp. "Some wedding, with no booze."

176

"You know how Mormons are."

"Don't care to," she said and shook out a cigarette. "Heard you graduated college."

"Yeah, a couple months ago."

"Working anywhere?" she said, lighting her cigarette.

"Yeah ... the adult mart out on the highway."

Aunt Miriam had been inhaling, now she went into a coughing, laughing fit.

"Now, that's funny," she said when she'd hacked up her lung. "I'd heard it, but wanted to see if it was true."

"Who told you? Mom?"

"She don't tell me shit. Your uncle Bob said it, I think."

"I thought you and Mom were back on good terms," I said.

"Eh."

I took another swig and offered it back to Miriam. We watched the dancers together. Dustin and Esmerelda danced in the middle of the floor, looking into each other's eyes. I wondered if I'd ever find something like that, or if I even wanted to.

Joey was still dancing with Mom. He spun her around. He really was a good dancer. And Mom was keeping up, really moving with him. Wiggling her hips, twirling her fingers in the air. With how much she ragged on him around me and Trish.... Now she seemed completely under his spell.

Trisha was dancing in a circle with Kevin and some other cousins around some guy who'd unbuttoned his shirt and was busting a move to "Groove Is in the Heart." Trish kept looking over at Joey and Mom, though, in a watchful way, like she was more fascinated with Joey than she was sure of him. Like I was,

177

I suppose.

"Empty," Miriam said, holding the flask out to me.

"I've got more in the car. Just need to reload."

"So ... you gonna make a career of the porn store?"

"No. Hopefully not."

"That's smart," she said, her voice muffled from the fresh cigarette she'd put in her mouth. She flicked a lighter and held it to the tip. Took a deep drag, hacked it out of her liquified lungs.

"I'm trying to move to New York City," I said.

"Oh, really," Miriam said.

"Yeah."

Miriam looked at me. Took another drag, which she didn't cough out. Shrugged. "Seems a folly," she said.

My defenses went up, but what she said felt true. My dream was gradually getting worn down to a Groom-sized nub. "Well, I don't have anything else to do," I said. "I can't stay here."

"Look at your Dad. He lived in Pittsburgh—not a huge city, but it ain't the sticks, either. He bummed around there for years. Wrote a book. Before your mother made him move here. That's what you wanna do, ain't it? Write books?"

"Make paintings," I said.

"You can do that anywhere," she said with a toss of her hand.

Joey walked toward us. The white lights around the arch made his damp forehead and chest gleam.

"Hello, handsome," Miriam said.

"Joey, this is my aunt. This is Trisha's boyfriend."

"I got that from the way you two was working it out on the dance floor," Miriam said.

"Nice to meet you," Joey said, shaking her hand. "Think I could bum a cigarette?"

Miriam regarded Joey. She seemed to take him in all at once. "Not from me, baby doll. I'm on a fixed income."

Joey chuckled, but I could tell he was put off. *He's used to getting what he wants*, I realized. "I'll just grab one from Trisha," he said.

"Yeah, get it from your girlfriend. You kids shouldn't be smoking anyway. Hey Nate—thanks for the drink."

"Any time, Aunt Miriam."

She walked away.

"Ain't she salty," Joey said. I could smell the liquor on his breath. We were both drunk. We were alone. "Our flask is empty. Can I have a swig of yours?"

"Mine's out, too. I gotta refill," I said.

"I'll come with you," Joey said.

Did I know what was going to happen at that moment? Sometimes it felt like we were in a car that was careening out of control. All it would've taken was for one of us to grab the wheel and steer us to safety, but neither of us were willing. We just sat in the back seat, enjoying the thrill of the ride, letting it take us where it did.

We walked into the dark field where the cars were parked. Stood next to Joey's car. I looked back at the wedding as Joey lit a cigarette. Mom was conversating. Miriam sat near her. Trisha danced with Kevin.

If anything is going to happen, it's going to happen now. Nobody is paying attention.

"I see you managed to charm my mom," I said.

"You think?" I looked at him, trying to suss out whether his naïveté was real or a put on.

"You got her to dance with you. I can't remember the last time I saw her dance."

"I like her." I almost said, *I bet you do*, but stopped myself. Why did I want to get aggressive about his relationship with *my mother*, of all people?

"Think I should fuck her?" he said.

"Gross," I said, but my anger was rising.

"I could just eat her out. I bet she hasn't had that done to her in a while."

I pushed him, meaning to be playful, but it was hard enough that he fell against his car. Had it not been there, I think he would've hit the ground. He looked at me, smirking, but surprised. I was shaking a little. Joey righted himself.

"Chill," he said.

"Sorry," I said, stuffing my anger.

Joey smirked. He took my hand, untucked his shirt, and rested my palm against his tight, smooth stomach. I felt stubble where his happy trail would've been.

"You shaved," I said.

"Mm hm," he said, looking in my eyes. He still had my hand by the wrist. He shoved it past his belt and into the front of his pants. No underwear, as usual. The smoothness of his stomach continued down into his pants until I found the root of his hard cock, trapped pointing downward against his slacks. All of it was smooth. He kept moving my hand downward until I felt his balls. "I shaved everything."

"Did you do it for her?" I said.

"Nope. I said I did it to surprise her. But really it was for you." He took my hand out of his pants and pulled me close into him. I heard the DJ switch songs, people cheering. Joey pushed my hand into the back of his pants. I felt his curved lower back, then his tight crack. I pushed my finger into it, against his hole. All shaved. "You know I'd never shave that for her. 'Cause it's yours."

"Fuck, Joey," I said. I was drunk. I nuzzled his neck, sank my fingers into his warm ass cheeks until they were knocking against his hole. It was so wrong, so dangerous. His asshole was moist.

"I lubed up in the bathroom just a minute ago," he whispered into my ear. "I want to do it here. I want you to fuck me here."

I pushed my finger inside of him. Joey kissed me, his tongue sliding against mine. Our breath was sharp with the whiskey we'd been drinking all night.

"We can't. Not here," I said.

Joey looked around. "Let's go into the woods," he said, jerking his head toward the crest of dark trees that ringed the field.

He started off. I followed. The land rose at the tree line, so we trudged upwards into the woods. The further we got, the less I could hear the music and the more I could hear the earthy sounds of summer in the forest—frogs, cicadas. I looked back. The pavilion, next to the shifty, watery light from the pool, looked like a mirage.

Joey sidled up to a tree and, smiling, undid his pants.

"Are we really gonna mess around here?" I said.

"Why not?" he said, dropping his pants. His cock sprung out, hard.

"Everybody's right there...."

"Exactly. They're over there. We're over here." He grabbed my cock through my pants. "I want you to fuck me." He turned around and braced himself against the tree. His pants were around his ankles. He lifted the tails of his shirt to reveal his ass, firm and glowing white in the moonlight. He arched his back, presenting it to me.

"All right. Just a quick one," I said. How could I resist when he made it so easy for me? I undid my fly, took out my cock, slid it in him just like that.

"Aw ... fuck me, shove that cock in me ... I want it so bad." He kept up a steady stream of dirty talk, but I could still hear the reception, faint on the night air, and could still see it off in the distance: people laughing, celebrating with family. And here I was in the woods, doing something nasty and secret. In my drunk mind, I had this vision of being cast out into these woods forever, the reception a utopia from which I'd been banished.

I pumped in and out of him, fucking him, my perfect cock in his perfect ass and both of us feeling it perfectly, the delicious, tight friction of his asshole massaging every inch of me, my cock a live wire of nerve endings, heady unthinking pleasure. Joey, my come brother, whose ass belonged to me and me alone, and couldn't I have this? Just this one thing?

I reached around to stroke his cock, but he knocked my

182

hand away. "Just use me, man. Just enjoy it." So, I held tight to his hips and fucked and fucked as hard as I wanted.

"Come in me, man. I want to have it in all night." I saw him dancing with my mom and my sister, my load dripping down his legs, saw him meeting members of my family and throwing his charm around and everyone saying, *What a nice guy.*

Joey kept talking. He was stroking himself now. "Doing it here, while they're all there...," he said, looking out at the wedding party, at my family.

"Fuck, I'm coming," I said. Losing it, blowing inside him, the blast of orgasm obliterating all for a lost moment until the earth settled and there I was....

"Oh man, I can feel it," he said. "I'm coming, too ... fuck!" He came all over the tree, and his eyes never left the crowd.

19

We got ourselves as presentable as we could, tucked in shirts and readjusted ties. Leaves and sticks crunched underfoot. At the edge of the woods, I paused. There were rows of cars just ahead of us, the reception a few yards beyond that. I had to go back there, act like I didn't have this burning secret, be normal. The prospect of it exhausted me.

"Thanks for that, buddy," Joey said, coming up behind me. He wrapped his arms around my back. It felt good. He nuzzled my neck, and I turned my head and kissed him.

We could run away together right now. Just get in the car and leave all this behind....

The slam of a car door. Joey and I pulled away from each other.

Aunt Miriam was staring at us. She was standing next to Joey's car with a flask in her hand—Trisha's flask, I would later come to understand, which she'd gone to refill. She stood stock-still, and the shock of it vibrated between us on an invisible wire. Her eyes were magnified by her thick glasses, and the moonlight glinting off of them were like high beams pointed in our direction, laying us bare before she turned and walked away.

I realized Joey was talking. "Did she see us? Dude, was that your aunt? Fuck, what was she doing up here? Do you think she saw us? Fuck, fuck, fuck...."

◆

Joey went ahead of me and I let him, figuring it wouldn't be a good idea for us to come back at the same time. I almost wanted to, though, wanted to come back holding hands and skipping through the grass, for fuck's sake, putting an end to this thing once and for all. Instead, I trudged along, my shoes sinking into the moist grass. No hurry, but my path inexorable.

My insides felt twisted. Joey strode toward the pavilion from the side, crept in. People probably hadn't even noticed he'd been gone. He was so good at that.

I stood next to the pool and watched him. He approached Trisha from behind, snaked his arms around her back. Her *face*—it lit up with the power of a million suns. Her boyfriend was there, only for her, and finally she could ignore the guy dancing in front of her, our second cousin twice-removed (or something) Danny, who was newly divorced and getting more lecherous as the night went on. Trisha pulled Joey in close, all trusting, no thought or clue about where he'd just been. The music changed. She swayed with him.

Aunt Miriam sat at a table a few feet away, watching them. As I watched, she stood, lifted her chair, and turned it away from them. She took a big drag off her cigarette and blew it into the air like the world deserved smoke in its face.

What can I say? I rejoined the party. I played like all was normal. Life went on as it almost always does. Planes crash into buildings and send them to the ground, for fuck's sake. The ice caps are melting more quickly than anybody previously predicted. Somebody just got diagnosed with terminal cancer, you lost your job, another mass shooting, another day.

My Aunt Miriam caught me kissing my sister's boyfriend. You stuff it down, you go on, you wait for the other shoe to drop and, in the meantime, you go back to the car and refill your flask.

When I got back to the dance floor, I'd sent a couple more sheets to the wind. Mom was still dancing. She was tipsy, too. She took my face into her hands.

"You're so handsome! Sometimes I see you and, for a minute, I think I see your father," she said.

"Aw, c'mon, Mom."

I sat for the rest of the reception, swigging from my flask, not caring who saw. I seemed to get more sober as I drank. People tried to get me to dance, but all I wanted to be was sitting at that table, nothing more, nothing less.

Aunt Miriam sat, too. Smoked cigarette after cigarette, her eyes darting all over the room, but never landing on me.

Joey kept dancing. Joey danced all night.

I woke up at Mom's, with no memory of getting into the car. I was in my old bedroom. I had to puke. I stumbled down the hall and made it to the toilet. I lay back down. The sun was beaming through the window right onto me. I felt like I'd been crushed under a truck. The room throbbed and waved. I tried to throw up again, but nothing came.

Mom made me a grilled cheese sandwich, which I managed to get down. I drank what felt like two gallons of water and fell back asleep. When I woke, I felt at least functional, which was good because I had to go to work.

Mom drove me. "What an interesting wedding," she said. "I would've expected things to be a bit more formal, but I suppose that's how people do things these days. Still, Dustin seemed happy with that girl."

"Esmerelda," I said.

"Whatever. They seemed happy. I guess that's the most important thing."

◆

I am not going to have sex with Joey anymore. Me at work, hardening my resolve.

Randy wasn't around that night. It was just me and the endless stream of pervs, people a lot like Joey, married men on the sly. I hated them. I hated the casualness of it, people who barely spoke to one another, barely looked at one another, doing something so intimate as going inside each other, depositing fluids into each other, slurping the germs off one another's bodies.

It was so fucking busy. I had to clean up piss literally three times that night. Even though I cleaned it with bleach, it still smelled like my Aunt Miriam's house, except this didn't come from cats. It came from a herd of horny men who couldn't take a moment to go outside and piss for fear that they might miss the perfect dick, ass, or mouth. I was nauseous still, and I had to sneak into the back alley to vomit once. Finally, Elton came in to relieve me, and it was time to go home.

I couldn't do it. For almost an hour, I just sat in the parking lot, under the yellow glow of the store sign, cars passing by, sometimes slowing to look at me. I didn't want to stay, but I didn't want to leave either.

A car parked, and Larry came out.

"Evening, sunshine," he said and sat next to me. "Want a cigarette?"

"Yeah," I said, looking up at him. His face was kind, and I knew that it wasn't the customers or the place, that I was projecting my disgust upon them for something that hit close to home.

"What's going on?" he said.

"I got caught," I said.

"Doing...," Larry said patiently.

"My sister's boyfriend."

"You're doing it with your sister's boyfriend?"

"Yeah," I said. Larry stared into my eyes with this really intense look. Then he stood and raised his hands to the sky.

"Praise Jesus," he said. I was startled. "Hallelujah. Oh, girl!" He leaned down to me, clutched my shoulders. "It's the holy grail of straight men! You have to tell me ... oh, I'm sorry," he said when he finally saw my face. "Oh, honey," he said and sat down again. "So, you got caught, huh?"

"*Yes*," I said.

"Your sister caught you."

"No. It was my aunt."

"And she *told* your sister?"

"No. Not yet."

"How do you know she's going to?"

"I guess I don't know," I said. Somehow—blame it on my hangover colluding with my shame—this had never occurred to me.

"Well...," Larry said, shrugging and sucking on his cigarette. "Where were you anyway that your *aunt* caught you?"

"At my cousin's wedding. We went into the woods."

Larry rolled his eyes and said, "I'm sorry, honey, but that is fucking *hot*," which made me smile. "But I understand that you're worried. You're living with her, right?" I nodded. "Well, if you need a place to stay the night, just until things cool off...."

"Thanks," I said, creeped out and touched just the same. "I'll be all right."

"Okay then," he said and stood. "I got a date with ... well, with whatever's going on in there tonight."

"It's busy," I said.

"Take some pictures next time," he said, the bell ringing as he swung open the door, and stepped inside the bright store.

I imagined seeing Trisha standing outside of her house, waiting for me with that dead look in her eyes, my stuff strewn about in the front yard. And then what would I do—go to Mom's? What if she was pissed at me, too? This idea of not having a home or a place to stay made me panic.

But when I got home, all was the same. The stoop was empty, the house dark and quiet—they'd already gone to bed. Trisha had left the little light above the stove on for me like she always did. I ate leftover wedding cake for dinner and went to bed.

Whump, whump, whump.

I woke to the sound. But then he came out of the bedroom door. "Hey. Good morning," he said.

"Were you just upstairs?" I said.

"No," he said. *Strange.* "Why?"

"I thought I heard you."

He shook his head. "Do you *want* to go up there?" he said, raising his shirt to reveal his flat stomach. At the same time, he lowered his shorts to show the shaved mound of his crotch. "I'd be down for it ... I'm always down."

"No ... don't you remember what happened at the wedding?"

"What happened?" he said, dropping his shirt. His cock was getting hard. So was mine. I ignored it.

"We got caught." *Am I going crazy?* "By my aunt. Remember?"

"Oh. Do you really think she saw us?"

"Yes," I said.

"Well, who knows if she'll even say anything." He plopped down onto the easy chair, like the weight of my questions was more than he cared to bear. "You said she doesn't even talk to your mom, right?"

"No, they talk. I think."

"Well, Trisha didn't say anything. Nobody's in trouble yet."

"So...."

"So, let's go upstairs," he said, raising his eyebrows.

"Joey," I said. He had a tendency to wince whenever I addressed him by name. "Don't you think we ought to quit

190

while we're ahead? If she finds out, we'd both be fucked. You'd lose your girlfriend. I'd lose my sister."

Joey nodded, all but shrugged. "I mean, it was pretty dark. She seemed practically blind," he said.

"You seem blind."

"What's that mean?"

"I can't do it anymore! It's too stressful. I get sick about it sometimes. Don't you?"

"Nope," he said.

I turned my head from him. I wanted to fight with him. I wanted something to blow up so that I wouldn't have to make a decision.

"So, you don't want to mess around anymore. Not even one more time, like a send off?" He had his hands down the front of his shorts. He watched me watch him as he fiddled around in there, then he lowered his shorts to reveal his hard cock. There was a gleam of pre-come at the tip. "What if we just jacked off together?"

"You really think it would just be that?"

Joey shrugged. He didn't care. Why did I care?

"It could be whatever we want," he said. "Who cares about anything else? It's just us right now. Nobody else is here. Nobody else is gonna know what we do at this moment." I found it hard to ignore his logic, amongst other things. He stroked his cock, watched me. "You know you want it in you. Come over and have a seat."

"No," I said and got up. "I can't. I'm gonna take a shower."

"I'm gonna jack off."

"Well, it's your house," I said.

"Otherwise, I'll be horny all day."

"You're horny all day anyway."

"Yep," he said, and I retreated to the bathroom and locked the door.

I jacked off in the shower. I tried to avoid thoughts of Joey as I did it, like banishing him from my jack-off fantasies was the first step. I thought of my ex, I thought of Nick, I thought of random, disembodied parts—anything that wasn't attached to my present situation. It wasn't easy. The first night with Eric in the dorm. The times spent between Nick's thick thighs in his attic bedroom. I felt up my smooth, soapy body, imagining my hand was someone else's, somebody I didn't know, somebody I had no history with, gliding across my hairless pecs and tight stomach, wrapping around the root of my hard cock, inching around my pelvis to my ass and traveling down my crack to my tight, horny hole....

The bathroom door opened.

"Dude, can I have some privacy?" I said.

"I just need to brush my teeth," he said.

"I thought I locked it."

"Guess you didn't," he said.

Locks didn't even work with Joey. I watched him from inside the shower, blurry peach-colored flesh and a white shirt on the other side of the translucent curtain, rummaging around the sink for his toothbrush and turning to look at the shape of me.

"Are you jerkin' off in there?" he said. I ignored it. He uncapped the toothpaste, squeezed some onto his brush, and closed the flip-cap with a pop. Stood there brushing his teeth, turning toward the mirror, then back around toward me. I washed myself halfheartedly, waiting for him to leave. My cock only got harder.

Joey spit, rinsed. "I can see your cock," he said. "You're hard." He pulled off his shirt and slid off his shorts.

"C'mon, Joey," was all I managed as he pulled back the curtain and let me see him in all his glory.

"I'm hard, too." He shifted his hips, made his cock wag back and forth like the tail of a happy dog. He stepped inside. I gave him room. He went under the spray. I watched the water cascade over his body.

He was right. Nothing had changed. Aunt Miriam hadn't told anybody, and fuck, maybe she really hadn't seen anything.

She did.

It wasn't like we could turn back time and erase all the sex we'd already had. I was already in. Shouldn't I just keep enjoying it if it was all going to blow up eventually anyway? If it even *was* going to blow up?

"C'mon," Joey said, taking my hand. He put it around his cock. "Nobody's gonna know." It was as hard and slick as a bar of soap. I stroked it up and down. "God, yeah," he said and kissed me, water streaming over our faces and lips. He grasped my sides and turned me around. "I'll clean your ass for you." He rubbed the bar of soap against my ass, then scrubbed me with his hand, rubbing his finger against the edge of my hole. He paused there, then pressed into it—not enough to make it go inside, but enough to make me feel it, pressure against my softest, most vulnerable spot.

"You want me in you?" he said.

"Yes."

"Say it."

"I want you to fuck me."

"Mm hm," he said and popped the tip of his finger inside me. Joey wrapped his other arm around my chest, holding me steady as he finger-fucked me. I relaxed into his embrace, into the invasion of his finger.

If this is the last time, I better make the most of it, I thought, and let it all go as Joey took out his finger and got into position behind me. He sank his cock into me just as easy as can be because it was easy with us. It was practiced and it was good. He fucked me and I fucked myself on him, both of us rocking underneath the spray of the shower, enjoying the feel of connection and abandon.

I made the most of it. But it wasn't the last time.

20

I stopped at Mom's before I went to work that day. She was in the kitchen, canning tomatoes.

"What have you been up to, Mom?"

"What do you mean?" she said.

"I don't know. I was just ... wondering what you've been up to."

"You mean since I saw you yesterday? Nothing, that's what. Picking tomatoes. Borrowing these jars off of Donna, not that that was a picnic. You'd think I was asking to borrow a thousand dollars the way she acts about these jars."

All seemed kosher in Mom world, and my anxiety lessened a bit. I even helped her out, boiling and peeling tomatoes.

"That Joey sure is a good dancer," she said. "He's so handsome, too. Don't you think?"

"I guess you approve of him now?"

"Approve of him? When did I ever not?"

"Mom, you used to talk down about him all the time."

"No, I did not," she said.

"Okay...."

"I mean, I guess he could have a better job than doing construction, but he seems like a hard worker. And he really seems to love Trisha and treat her well."

"Well, he drives me nuts," I said.

"In what way?"

"I don't know. Just living with him ... he's not real clean,"

I said lamely.

"Well, neither are you," she said.

I rinsed the jars she had set up on the counter. "Aunt Miriam talked to me quite a bit at the reception," she said. The jar I was rinsing under the faucet slipped out of my hands and went clattering into the aluminum sink. It didn't break.

"Oh yeah?" I said, trying to act nonchalant.

"Mostly when we first got there. She seems well. Her emphysema is under control. I don't know for how long, with all the smoking she does. Did you talk to her?"

"A little bit."

"Hm," she said.

"I thought you guys weren't really on speaking terms."

"We hadn't been. Not for a year, maybe. But who knows. I might give her a call one of these days," she said, ladling boiling tomatoes from the pot and into a jar—heart-like, fleshy bulbs to seal off for the winter.

I sat with Trisha in the morning, drank the coffee that she offered to me.

"Christ, I just want to sleep in. I wish I could call off," she said.

"Don't you have sick days?"

"Yeah, but it's a crazy week. We're doing our annual internal audit."

"So what? That's what sick days are for. I wish I could call off sometimes," I said.

196

Trisha took a sip of coffee. "Have you saved much? Summer's, like, practically over," she said.

"August just started. Anyway, I've got over a grand saved."

"You know you can't live here forever."

"I know," I said.

"Not to be mean. It's just, you know, Joey and I wouldn't mind having the place to ourselves soon. That was the idea behind moving in together to begin with. Not that you're a huge imposition or anything. Lord knows you probably see Joey more than I do." She took another sip, gazed at the gray light coming in through the window. "That wedding got me thinking," she said, a smile coming across her face.

"Really?" I said.

"Do you think he'd marry me?"

"Joey?"

"No," she said sarcastically, leveling her gaze at me. I shrugged. "We've talked about it. Sort of. I don't think he'd ever asked me, though. I guess it's weird to ask him, but I might do it."

"I don't know, Trish. You're still pretty young. He's like your first real boyfriend."

"I've had lots of boyfriends," she said, setting down her cup.

"I guess so...." I said. *He's the first one who's fucked you properly, is what you're thinking. But there are more of them out there, surely there are, good looking guys with jobs who can fuck good and who won't fuck your brother at the same time.*

"But he's like your first serious one," I said.

"That's what I mean. It's different with him," she said,

197

pulling her hair back into a ponytail and securing it with an elastic band. I didn't like the way she was looking at me, with this hardened resolve, like her decision to marry gave her a maturity that I couldn't understand, like the fact that I was suspicious only reinforced her decision to do it.

"It'd make Mom happy, anyway. She loves him now, for some reason," I said.

"I don't know why you care."

"Well, you asked."

"Still. You guys get along. I'd think you'd want him around," she said.

"I didn't say I cared. Do whatever you want," I said.

Trisha stood. She picked up her empty cup, and then grabbed mine. Before I could say anything, she emptied it into the sink.

"Thanks," I finally said. "I wasn't done with that."

Trisha didn't say anything. An uncomfortable silence grew between us, as it seemed to do more and more lately. I'd never experienced this before. Sometimes I couldn't think of a single thing to say to her. Into the silence would rush guilt and shame, which made it even harder to get back to our usual banter.

She left. He arrived. Out of the bedroom, anyway. He was stark naked and had a hard-on. He paused in the doorway, stretching his arms over his head, yawning.

"Morning," he said, smiling at me. Then he strode to the bathroom, seemingly uninterested in my reaction, or maybe just sure of it. His cock bounced, his firm ass flexed as he made his way into the bathroom. I heard the shower turn on.

I thought about leaving. Going to Mom's. Hell, even going

to work and just hanging out. But it became a thing. I was going to stick around and have the willpower not to do anything.

Joey came out of the bathroom a half hour later, only half hard now. I tried to keep my eyes on the TV as he poured a bowl of cereal and sat in the chair. When he finished eating, he sat his bowl on the coffee table. He stretched again, spreading his legs, his cock lolling to one side and resting on his thigh. He groaned as he stretched. He was trying to get my attention, and he'd finally got it.

"Are you gonna put on some clothes today?" I said.

"Does it bother you?"

"No," I said. Saying "yes" would have felt like an acknowledgement of the war that was going on in my head, which we were both aware of and which he, frankly, was winning. My cock was hard in my shorts. Luckily it was hidden by the blanket over my lap.

"Okay. Then no, probably not. Too hot," he said.

"Well, what would Trisha think if she came back and saw you like that?"

Joey lit a cigarette, sat back. "She'd probably get horny."

I rolled my eyes.

"What are you doing today?" he asked.

"I don't know. I have to work. I might go for a walk," I said.

"And you don't want to fuck. Right?"

"Right. I'm sorry."

Joey shrugged. "Whatever," he said. "You wanna smoke? I just got some really good stuff off Bev. You gotta try it."

Sex and drugs: my vices from that summer.

"Sure," I said.

Joey smirked. We both knew what was going to happen once we got high, even if he was the only one willing to acknowledge it. He went into the bedroom, came out in a pair of shorts with a baggy and his glass pipe.

"Let's go smoke out back," he said.

I followed him down the hall and out the back door. He grabbed a blanket that Trisha had folded up on the chaise lounge and spread it on the grass, right in a patch of hot morning son. I sat next to him as he packed the pipe. Joey sparked the pipe and handed it to me. I took a deep hit and let it out.

We passed it back and forth. Sometimes our fingers got tangled. I got high, higher. It was really good weed. He took a deep hit. "C'mere," he said through held breath, beckoning me with his fingers. I came closer. "Shotgun," he said and brought his mouth to mine. He breathed out and I breathed in, taking in his smoke. I held it. My eyes were closed, the sun sieving through my eyelids, a veiny red glow. Joey's face was close. He put his lips on mine and kissed me. I broke away, turned my head just to the side, exhaled. Pulled his head to mine and shoved my tongue in his mouth.

Was there ever any doubt? I thought as he laid me back into the grass and rested his body on top of mine. The weight of him was both sexy and comfortable. *Why do you do this to yourself? Deny what you're going to eventually succumb to anyway?*

We made out in the soft breeze. Joey slipped my shorts off, then his. We were naked outside, hard and in lust for each other. He spun around, took my cock into his mouth, and lowered his cock into mine. I grabbed his ass. He did the same. Clutching each other, fingers roaming deeper. It was the hottest sixty-nine I'd ever had, both of us wanting each other's cocks and come, wanting whatever we could give one another. No limits. No holds barred.

I slipped my tongue in his ass and he did the same, wrapping my arms around his hips and straining to dig as much of myself in him as he was in me. When he slipped a slick finger into me, I did the same to him.

Me in you and you in me. Come brothers. I took his cock in my mouth again, sucking him as I sunk my finger deeper into his ass. He fixed a second finger into me. We were working toward it. We were going to come in each other's mouths, come at the same time, the ultimate expression of our bond, which was after all just body parts in other body parts, fluids inside orifices.

Come brothers. Something deeper than a familial bond? Something different and, fuck, if it didn't feel worth it sometimes, like something I'd yearned for all my life, something that made me want to say fuck her and fuck their relationship and fuck my relationship with her because *this is mine.* I want this. I'm taking this. It's just for me, only for me, and it's nobody's business but ours.

We didn't come, though, because we heard my mom's voice coming from inside the house.

21

"Nate?" Mom said. "Joey?"

I remember thinking it wasn't real. The idea of my mom in my sister's house was alien, impossible. She'd never visited, as far as I knew.

It seemed like we just kept going for a moment, pumping fingers into asses, cocks into throats, orgasms imminent. The come-brother bond about to adhere.

"Joey?" she said, her voice nearer now. Did he pull me in a little closer then? It couldn't have happened like that. We were writhing on a blanket in the grass, and my mom was coming closer.

"Nate, are you home? I brought you all some sauce."

Maybe we were coming apart when it registered, when I heard her voice stop mid-sentence. "Are you—."

Something crashed inside the house. She was there, staring out through the screen door to where Joey and I were extricating ourselves from one another in what felt like slow motion. Fingers out of holes, mouths off of locked-and-loaded cocks. I looked at her and I knew that my dream had been a prediction after all, but it wasn't Trisha's dead-shock eyes I'd seen. It was my mom's eyes, shining in the dark of the house, glazed by the summer light.

Joey seemed to panic then because he tried to stand up quickly, swinging his leg around my head so that his foot whacked me in the face. I stood. Joey stood next to me. I covered my cock with my hands. Joey didn't, and even though his face was horrified, he seemed to spread his legs to give her a better look. Maybe I just remember it like that.

Mom made a sound halfway between a gasp and a gut punch. I pulled the edge of the blanket to cover myself, but Joey was still on it. He stepped off. I pulled up the blanket and wrapped it around my waist. She was gone, though.

I stood there in the sun and felt like I was underwater, Joey's panicked voice barely filtering through. "Oh fuck, she really saw. Fuck, how didn't we hear her? Fuck. What was she doing here? Do you think she's gonna say something? Nate? Nate?"

I walked toward the house, away from him. I wanted him to get swallowed up by the yard, the trees. I didn't want to have to hear him anymore. The patio cement burned the soles of my feet. I opened the screen door. Big, blood-red puddle on the floor, a smashed jar of sauce, thick chunks of clear glass in it.

Step in it. Eat it. Cut yourself with it.

I stepped over it. Went through the living room and into the kitchen. The front door was open. Joey's car was in the driveway. I thought I heard a car driving up into the woods. Mom's? Regardless, she was gone.

I felt cold. Numb. I wrapped the blanket tighter around me and sat at the kitchen table.

"Nate, are you okay? What are we gonna do? Nate, talk to me. Dude, are you all rright?"

I just rocked back and forth, ignored him until he finally went into the bedroom.

It seemed like it was time to leave for work just a few minutes later. In reality, it was a few hours. Somehow I wound up dressed, and so did Joey. I cleaned up the sauce. Joey talked the entire time. I'd never known him to talk so much, like he was holding up both ends of a conversation we should be having. I could barely think, let alone articulate.

"Maybe she won't say anything. She might not. She might just want to ignore it. Does she seem like the type who'd ignore it? She does, doesn't she? But she's gonna *have* to say something to her, right? Won't she?" I picked the shards of glass out of the sauce, sopped the rest up with a dish towel, and threw it into the washing machine, along with the blanket of Trisha's that I'd been sleeping with for the last eight weeks. I looked at my open suitcases. My clothes were spilling out of them and onto the floor. I packed them up. Packed everything I had into my two suitcases. Sat them next to each. Looked at them.

Joey was walking around in the attic. I wondered if he was packing, too. I checked before I left for work. He was lying on the attic sofa with headphones on, his eyes closed. He took off the headphones and looked up at me. I remember how young he looked just then.

"I'm going to work. I'm gonna just leave my stuff," I said.

"Your stuff?"

"I thought I might take my suitcases with me, but I can't."

"Dude, don't jump the gun," he said, sitting up and hanging his headphones around his neck. "You thought your aunt caught us last week and nothing came of that. She might not say anything."

He had a point. My mom was weird about sex. It was hard

to imagine her saying something to my sister about it. I could envision her burying her head in the sand, avoiding my gaze over dinner, but never mentioning it.

It didn't matter to me at that moment. I wanted it to be over.

"I'm going to work," I said again and turned away from him. Walked out of the house and left my suitcases sitting there.

It was a beautiful day.

It's over.

Relief. There was money in my bank account. My life had just gotten a swift kick in the pants, maybe the kick that it needed. Here it was. The rest of my life was about to start, whether I liked it or not.

It's not over. The best part is, maybe. Now comes the worst.

Randy was working. He was harried.

"Rita walked out on her fucking shift. Locked up the store and walked out. Can you believe it? That asshole. I had to come in when Larry called to tell me the store was closed. Now I have to figure out how to dock her paycheck for the days she didn't work. Damned if I give her a cent more than she deserves. I knew I shouldn't have hired her. What a goddamned drama."

I set my bag behind the counter, clocked in. Randy's ranting was soothing to me at that moment. I let it wash over me. "I have to do the drop 'cause she didn't do it. We'll see if I can get to the damn bank in time. At least she didn't steal anything." Finally, he looked at me. "I'm sorry. How are you? You seem ... oh shit, what's wrong? What happened?"

"My mom caught us."

"You and the boyfriend?" he said.

"Yep."

"When?"

"Just earlier."

"How?"

"She saw us. In the backyard. We were ... on each other in the backyard, and she looked out and saw us."

"Oh, Nate." He sat on the stool next to me, put his hand on my shoulder. "That is most unfortunate."

"I don't know what I'm going to do," I said. Just acknowledging that made me start to panic. The relief I'd felt on the way to work was gone. I couldn't breathe, and then I was crying, but it was more like I was choking. I stood up and doubled over. I got on the floor.

Randy got down with me. He held me by the shoulders. "It's not the end of the world. I'm sure it feels like it, but it's really not." He kept on like that, comforting me, until Lloyd came in and he got up to sell him his tickets.

"You all right?" Lloyd said, looking at me on the floor. I tried to smile.

"He'll be okay," Randy said. Lloyd nodded. His eyes were magnified by his thick glasses. When he blinked, they looked like camera shutters snapping. He walked into the back. I wondered if he had a sister, if they were close, if he was the type of person to do something like I did.

"Tell me again how you fucked your sister's boyfriend," I said.

"Fiancé," Randy said and sat down next to me. "They were engaged."

"How did that happen?"

"It was so long ago. I was just a kid—younger than you are even. And Dom, well … he wasn't much older either. Like I said, he didn't know he was gay until we got together. I was his first."

"Did he seduce you?"

"Hm. No. We just … came together," he said.

"How did she find out?"

"Dom told her. He knew he had to."

"Joey's not going to do that," I said.

"Right," Randy said. He stretched his legs out in front of him. The heels of his shoes skittered across the gritty linoleum.

"I feel like I wish we were in love. It would make me less of a monster," I said.

"Well, if he's not in love with you, chances are he's not in love with her either."

"I think she's in love with him, though."

"Could be," Randy said. He put his arm around me and pulled me into him. "Everything's going to be okay. Not that that makes it any easier. But the burden of betrayal lies with him, ultimately."

I stood. Randy stood with me. He looked around the store. "Christ, now I'm gonna have to hire somebody else. I'm so tired of dealing with this dump." He walked over to Sylvia the mannequin. I watched him consider her, then he walked to the dildo aisle.

"What are you doing?" I said.

"Something I've been wanting to do ever since I bought this place and inherited that stupid fucking mannequin." He took a rubber dong with a suction-cup base out of its plastic package.

It was rainbow-colored, thick as a can of beans and two-baby-arms long. He lifted Sylvia's fishnet dress and suctioned it right to her Barbie-doll crotch. It bobbed heavily, but stuck.

"We should put a ball gag on her face," I said.

"Now you're talking."

I unboxed a Tweety Bird ball gag and strapped the yellow rubber ball to her puffed-up lips. The *pièce de résistance* was the pocket pussies we fitted onto her fingers and toes.

"She's beautiful," Randy said as we stood back and admired our handy work. He turned to me. "So, you're staying at my place tonight."

Man, what a relief it was to hear that. My shift went by in a daze, and when it was over, Randy picked me up and took me to his house. He heated some leftovers, and I sat at his table and ate while he changed the sheets in his extra bedroom. I thought I'd have a hard time sleeping, but it was just the opposite: As soon as I lay down on his soft bed, the food settling in my stomach, I crashed.

In the morning, Randy made us breakfast, then we sat on the couch in our pajama pants and watched old movies, which only half-distracted me. By noon, I got the courage to turn on my phone. I'd missed a call from my mom. She hadn't left a message.

I steeled myself and went to the back porch to call her. She picked up on the second ring.

"Hi, honey," she said. I don't know what I expected, but it hadn't been the warmth that was in her voice.

"Mom," I said. She let out a deep breath. "I'm sorry you saw that, Mom."

"I am, too." We were both silent for a few awkward moments. "Honey, what was that? I'm not sure I understand."

"Well, Joey and I ... we've been, kind of, doing stuff together—"

"Does Trisha know?"

"No! No." I said. What was she thinking? That Trisha and I had some understanding? Share and share alike?

"Is he gay? Joey?" she said.

"I don't think so, Mom. I think he's bisexual." Mom was quiet. I suspect bisexuality wasn't something she could process.

"Why would you do something like that, Nate?"

"It just happened, Mom."

"Well, I don't want to know anything else about it. Are you there right now?"

"No, I'm at Randy's house. So, you didn't tell her?"

"No," she said. "He just ... he seemed like a nice boy. He seemed so good for her."

"He's not that great, obviously," I said.

"Well, I just didn't expect this from him."

"Did you expect it from *me*?"

"Oh, come on now. Don't try to pick a fight," she said. I *did* want to fight with her, to challenge her on her assumption that I would naturally do something depraved while the rest of the world wouldn't. But I didn't have a lot of ground to stand on at that moment.

"Look, Mom, don't say anything to her. I mean, I think I should tell her myself." The idea had just occurred to me, and even though I couldn't imagine myself doing it, somehow, I knew I had to. And that my mother shouldn't. "I think it should come from me."

"No, Nate. Don't … don't do that. Think about it first."

"Well, what is there to think about? Are we just going to keep this a secret from her for the rest of our lives? Let her marry Joey, turn a blind eye?"

"I just think you should consider how much it would hurt her."

"I know it's going to hurt her...."

"Nate, you can stay here. Why don't you come stay here? Instead of at your … well, that porn manager's place."

"I'm fine here, Mom." She huffed. "I'm going to go now, Mom. Please don't tell her."

"Well, I don't know."

"I'm asking you not to."

"Okay," she said. "I have to go."

"Allright. Bye," I said. And she hung up.

Randy was taking down some Christmas lights from the hallway. "She didn't tell her," I said. He nodded. "What am I going to do? Call up my sister, tell her I've been fucking her boyfriend for months? How the fuck.../"

"Well, really, it's Joey who needs to say something."

"But it's the right thing to do, right? I mean, especially now that our mother is involved."

"Probably," Randy said.

"What do you mean?"

"Well, I guess I don't know that telling her *is* the right thing to do. You doing it might be self-serving."

I was more confused than ever. I spent all day watching TV to distract myself, but kept a wary eye on my cell phone. My stuff was still at Trisha's, packed up and ready, and I hadn't been around for over a day. She had to have noticed.

Randy and I walked to the cemetery that evening, which suited my mood. Fuck whistling past the graveyard. Dom's grave was simple. There was a spot right next to it for Randy, which was weird to me.

"How long were you guys together?" I asked.

"Thirty-three years. It's rare, that's for sure."

"How'd you make it work?"

"We fucked other people," Randy said in all seriousness. "It's true. But it wasn't just that. We both wanted the same thing, when it came down to it—someone to spend the rest of our lives with. Well, he got what he wanted at least."

We went to my dad's grave.

"I always forget that you're Pat Audley's son," Randy said.

"Did you know him?"

"No, just of him. I've always meant to read his book."

"I don't think many people knew him. He didn't have any friends. Christ, we barely knew him ourselves," I said.

"I think a lot of dads are like that. It's cool that he left something behind for you, though. Like a legacy."

We fell asleep on the couch together when we got back to Randy's house. I wound up snuggling against him, my head on his thigh. He put his arm on my shoulder. It felt good.

22

Randy worked with me the next day. He justified it by saying he had stuff to catch up on, but I think he just wanted to keep me company. He changed the DVD selections for the booths, which was this laborious process of selecting two movies from all the various categories we had—black, bi, trans, gonzo—and loading them into thirty-two separate DVD players in the back office.

Larry came in halfway through. "How's the selection back there? Anything worth getting my makeup smeared?"

I shook my head. "Just old Lloyd holding down the fort."

Larry rolled his eyes. "*That* one. Have you ever seen his cock? It's a sight, really. One of the nicest cocks I've ever seen. Like a salami on steroids."

"How did you see it?" I said.

"What do you think it is back there, a nunnery?"

"Did you ... *do* anything with it?" I said.

"Oh, for god's sake. I do possess self-respect, you know. Not a lot, but...." He fished in his bag for a cigarette. "Guess I'll get my fix before the hunt."

"Randy's back there," I said.

"Oh good. She owes me twenty bucks for the Diana Ross tickets." Larry turned his head. A car was pulling into the parking lot. A maroon Cadillac. "Well, let's see what we have here...."

"Oh, man," I said.

Larry looked at me. "Someone you know?" Joey got out of the car and walked up to the glass door. My chest heaved with a familiar internal struggle: guilt and lust taking turns fondling the baton as they jogged beside each other, the best of bros. The fucker still looked sexy as hell, and I still wanted him. He had a smirk on his face as he opened the door and strode inside.

"Unf," Larry said. Joey sauntered up to the counter, his eyes roaming around the store, taking it all in.

"Hey Nate," Joey said.

"Hey Joey."

Joey looked to his left, at Larry who'd been staring at him the whole time.

Larry held out his hand. "Hello there, handsome," Larry said.

"Hey," Joey said, shaking Larry's hand. I cringed, anticipating a crack about how Larry had heard a lot about him, but he didn't go there.

"Well. Seems like you two need to talk, so I'm gonna go smoke this cigarette," Larry said and he walked out.

"What are you doing here?" I said.

"I need to talk to you. You haven't been around."

"Okay," I said. We were the only people in the store, but he still leaned in, whispered.

"I've been freaking out, Nate. I didn't know if your mom said anything to her or if you did."

"Neither of us did," I said.

"It's weird. I feel like she knows. She keeps asking about you, where you are."

"I'll have to come get my stuff eventually, I guess."

"Why'd you leave your bags like that? She hasn't tried to call you?"

"I don't know. No," I said.

"So that's it? You're moving out?" he said.

"Yeah. I mean ... I don't know. I'm staying away because I need to figure it out. I talked to my mom and asked her not to say anything for now."

Joey let out his breath. He leaned onto the counter. "Oh man, what a relief," he said.

I could smell him, some particular deodorant that would for the rest of my life remind me of him. I thought of what Randy said, that it might not be my place to end things, to tell Trisha. Like, if my mom didn't even want to do it, why should I? Joey wasn't bothered by it, so why should I be?

He looked toward the dark cavern that was the entrance to the booths. "So, what's back there anyway? Is that where people, you know, *fuck around*?"

"Yeah."

"Can *you* go back there?"

"C'mon, Joey. I'm working."

He stood up, casually slipped a hand under his shirt, enough to lift it beyond the waistband of his shorts to show a flat strip of his belly. "I know. But can you?" he said.

Randy came out from the back, his arms loaded with DVDs. He stopped. Looked at me. Looked at Joey. Sized up the situation in an instant.

"Hello there, sir," he said to Joey. "How are you today?"

"Good," Joey said.

"Let me know if I can help you find anything," he said,

winked at me and walked away.

"How much is it to go back there?" Joey said.

"Five bucks."

"Okay," he said, reaching into his pocket and pulling out a twenty. "Give me five then."

I rang him up, and he sauntered into the back with one final, pointed glance back at me. I let out my breath.

Randy walked up to the counter. "Oh man, he is fucking hot. Jesus Christ, no wonder."

Larry came back in. "Motherfucker," he said, grabbing both of my forearms. "Nate!" He looked like he'd just seen the cock of God. "Why are you not in the back?" He turned to Randy. "Did you see that?"

"That's some prime beef, indeed. But Nate's conflicted."

"I'm drooling. Drooling! And not from my mouth," Larry said.

"Ha!" Randy said.

"Go back there. Or I will," Larry said. They both looked at me expectantly.

"Fine," I said and headed around the counter.

"You'd think we told her to fold the laundry," Larry said.

"He's trying to be good," Randy said.

"Nate, darling, live a little. The time is now."

"I'm going!" I said and walked into the back. I told myself that I wasn't going to fool around with him. I was just going to talk to him, to figure out what to do next. I went past the two lit-up marquees and into the dim maze of black-painted partitions. I found Joey wandering around near the back. Lloyd was hot on his heels.

215

Joey smiled when he saw me. He ducked into the nearest booth and I followed. "Show me how this works. Man, this place is kinda sleazy, huh?"

"Exactly," I said, squeezing in beside him. It was tight quarters, but I wasn't about to sit on the bench, not after what I'd seen in that place.

"I don't even know what I'm stepping in here," Joey said, looking at his foot as he lifted it off the black floor.

"It's come, Joey. You're stepping in come."

"Oh man," he said. I asked for his paper coupons, and he handed them to me. Then I fed them into the machine and the TV popped on. "You dial it to whatever porn you want. There are thirty-two channels. Joey flipped around till he got to a male/male/female threesome.

"Nice," he said. We stood there watching it. I didn't know what I was doing. Apparently, we didn't have anything to say to one another. It smelled like come and piss. Joey started rubbing his crotch. He looked at me.

"I can't do anything back here. It's too weird," I said.

"That's okay," Joey said. "I know things are weird right now for you."

I got sad all of a sudden. Was it really over? The best sex of my life? It wasn't like I'd been in love with the guy, but we'd had a connection. And what was going to happen now? Just toss it out and try to forget about it?

Joey said, "I just wanted to check the store out. And I wanted to see you." He turned his body toward mine, reached down and took my hand.

"Thanks, Joey," I said. We moved closer to one another.

216

Blown-out moans from the ancient television system echoed throughout the dark space beyond the partition.

"Can I kiss you?" Joey said.

"Okay," I said, thinking, *It's just a kiss. Just for now, just for us.*

I loved making out with Joey. His lips were soft and his tongue was never too aggressive. We had this perfect symmetry when it came to kissing, which had been there from the start. For almost fifteen minutes, we stood in that back booth, making out. I saw people out of the corner of my eye, heard them shuffling around, poking their head in to see, to watch. But Joey and I kept at it. We never got distracted. I began to hold on to it, to feel like I might never have it again, to embrace it as a respite from all my anxiety, even if it was really the cause. Our cocks were hard, but we never grabbed them. We barely even bumped them against one another.

Finally, we came apart. Neither of us said much as we came out of the back. I walked him out to his car. We both scanned the highway like Trisha might drive by at any moment, which wasn't totally ridiculous. Groom is a small town.

"Are you gonna come back to the house soon?" he said.

"I'll have to."

"Do it soon 'cause she's starting to wonder," he said.

"Can I text you?" I said.

"No. I think she checks my phone. But come by. Especially if you hear anything from your mom." That was it. We said goodbye, waved awkwardly. Randy and Larry were waiting for me at the counter. I guess they'd both taken a peek at us in the back.

"That was beautiful," Randy said.

"That was hot," Larry said.

Randy wrapped his hand around the back of my neck. "You okay?" he said.

"I'm okay," I said.

"You can stay with me for as long as you want, you know. In fact, if you want to stay here past the summer, keep working at the store ... I'd make you a manager, give you some more money. You could take some more time to save up for whatever you want to do next."

"Thanks, Randy," I said. I wasn't sure what to make of the suggestion. It comforted and disturbed me equally.

◆

That night at Randy's, I got stoned and, as sometimes happens with weed, I got muddled clarity. I got on my laptop and bought a bus ticket to New York City. It left in ten days. I got on Craigslist and found several people who were looking for roommates. Most of the cheaper places weren't in Manhattan, but I'd already figured that I'd end up in Brooklyn or Queens. I did some financial figuring out and began to feel on top of things.

What had gone wrong? I'd done something stupid for one summer and, so far, nothing had come of it. I called my mom, but she didn't pick up. I started walking to Trisha's house. I figured I'd grab my bags and tell her that I was living with Randy now. No real reason, just to get out of their hair, done deal.

I guess the weed started to wear off about halfway there, and with it went my clarity and my courage. I started up the road to Trisha's house and noticed something sitting on the steps. Some trash, I told myself, but I had a sinking feeling.

They were my bags, set out where the trash would normally go. Her car was in the driveway. Joey's wasn't. What was somehow most awful was how carefully my bags had been placed there at the curb, the two of them sitting perfectly upright like patient children, zipped, just waiting for me to pick them up, move along, not even pause.

So, I didn't. I grabbed them and lugged them the two miles home like it was my penance.

My phone rang halfway to Randy's. It was my mom. I set my bags in the grass off the side of the road and sat on them. It was dark out now.

I answered. "So, you told her," I said.

"I had to do it," she said. She was crying. "It was just eating me up. Oh, honey, I hope you understand."

"I do," I said, though I wasn't sure if I did. "I'm just getting my bags from her place."

"Oh no. Don't go there."

"No, I just left there. She left my bags out," I said.

"Well, she doesn't want to see you. She was very clear about that. She didn't believe me at first...."

"Mom, I really don't want to know."

"Well, I hope that you two can have a relationship one day in spite of what you've done."

I started to feel annoyed with her. I tamped down my emotions. I guess I felt I didn't have a right to them, even though it seemed to me that she really didn't have a place in this, that she'd inserted herself somewhere where her actions and opinions were not welcome. But how could I say that when she was absolutely right about the fact that I'd fucked up, that I'd betrayed my sister—her daughter—in a tremendous way?

"Forgiveness doesn't always come easily, but I think she'll be able to find it for you," she continued.

"What are you talking about?" I said.

"Excuse me?" she said. I was sitting there under a sodium streetlight, and the bugs were swirling around, cars passing, the headlights illuminating me like I was a sideshow, sitting on my bags, clearly not in a good place. Maybe each of them felt better about themselves as they passed, grateful that they weren't in my place.

"You're acting like you're speaking for Trisha," I said. "It's up to her. All of this is. You don't have anything to do with it. Mom, I asked you not to tell her."

"What was I supposed to do? Keep that from my only daughter, let her marry a man like that? Let her go on thinking her brother cared about her when he really was *sleeping with her boyfriend*? I'm a better person than that."

"No, you're a selfish person," I said.

"Excuse me?"

I didn't have a response. It had just come out of me. It felt true, but I didn't have the footing to explain why.

It knocked the air out of mom. She sputtered for a second. "I c-can't believe you're acting all high and mighty after doing what you did...."

"I have to go," I said.

"I'm a good person," she said, and I could hear her crying now. "I never put demands on you, and you do whatever you want, *just like your father*."

I hung up. I turned off my phone.

I guess what hurt the worst was knowing what it must feel like for Trisha to have to hear about that from our mom, the embarrassment of having a relationship stumble right before her eyes.

I wanted to talk to Trisha about all of it. I wanted to laugh with her about it, the way we'd laughed when everything was at its craziest. We would laugh about my mom, after Dad's death, because it was one way to deal with it. Like the time she baked me a cake for my seventeenth birthday. It had been this huge thing, that she was going to bake me a cake, because my dad had been the cook in the family, and since his death, my mom had struggled with it. But this cake became her mission, and it seemed like in the weeks leading up to my birthday, every goddamned day she was picking up something else to make it with. Or I had to drive her places to get things for it. I put as much into making that cake as she did.

It ended up a disaster. She'd made not a sheet cake, not a two-layer cake—no, she'd attempted four layers. And the icing hadn't been from a tub. It had been homemade and made too thin, so that the layers slid out from under each other when she'd tried to ice it. One had slid right onto the floor. She wound up with a half-iced thing that looked like a Dali painting. Mom had been beside herself. But it had been *my* birthday, the whole time. My birthday, but her emotions, her show.

221

I was off work the next day, but I was so freaked out over everything that I finally just went to the porn store. I wanted to be around people, and I knew Randy was working.

I got halfway down the street when Joey's car pulled up next to me. My heart sank.

"Get in," he said.

"Why?"

"I need to talk to you."

"I didn't tell her."

"You didn't?"

"Our mom did," I said.

His expression changed, softened. "Will you just get in?" he said.

I did. We cruised off down the street and out of the main part of town. There was soft music coming from the radio—Pink Floyd. The inside of Joey's car made you feel like you were totally cut off from the world, a quiet and smooth oasis, and I found myself relaxing into it.

"Did she kick you out?" I said.

"Pretty much," he said. "All my stuff is still there, though."

"She put mine out on the street."

"Really?"

"Why is that surprising?" I said.

"I don't know. She didn't seem mad at you. She was really mad at me. She threw a box of cereal at me." I almost laughed. "But then we made up. We fucked."

"You *fucked?*"

222

"Yeah. Then after that, she told me to get out and not to come back until she said. I'm at my Dad's trailer now, but I can't stay there. I can't get hold of Bev." We drove up into the hills outside of town. It was getting dark.

"She didn't say anything about being pissed at me?" I said.

"Not really," he said.

"That's so weird."

"Look, I got a joint. What do you say we park somewhere and smoke it? I feel like we need it."

What can I say? We parked in a field off Derry Lane. We got out and smoked the joint and watched the sun dip below the horizon. When Joey went to kiss me, it felt exactly right. We fucked in the back seat, a desperate sort of fucking, a fuck to keep the demons at bay. I climbed on top of him, rode him steadily until I came all over his chest and he came inside me.

We got dressed and drove to the highway to get McDonald's, then we drove back to the field and ate it. We fucked again, this time me in Joey. I got aggressive, slapping his ass and really giving it to him. We came a second time, and then we curled up in the back seat. I held him as we drifted in and out of sleep.

His phone chirped. I looked at it. It was 6:00 a.m. I handed it to him. He rubbed his eyes as he stared at the screen.

"Shit," he said. "She wants me to come over."

I got dressed. The sun was starting to rise. He drove me to Randy's. I looked at him, cradling the steering wheel, gold chain around his neck, the crucifix lying on his shoulder.

"I wonder if I should try to contact her," I said.

"I don't know," he said. He seemed so dim to me just then. Why did I get so worked up over him? Why did my sister?

223

In my dad's book, the Martians live covertly, humans in disguise. They're overtaking the town, the world, by bringing people into their underground land, and they do that by seducing them, appealing to their most secret desires.

"I'll try to find you once I know what's going down," he said.

◆

Randy was making breakfast when I woke the next morning. I checked my phone. My sister had called and left a message. The notification icon on my screen said, "New Voice Mail" next to a cheery yet anxious-looking little envelope floating in space. I wanted to throw my phone into the garbage disposal, move my bus ticket up to that afternoon, and get out of town, never to talk to anybody again.

"She called you?" Randy said. "That's a good sign."

"You think?" I ate, then went into the backyard so that I'd have some privacy. I took a deep breath. Finally, I touched the little envelope, which connected me to my voice mail.

"One. New. Message."

Trisha's voice, flat and deep. "Nate, call me." It was impossible to tell anything from that. I disconnected from my voice mail, swiped through my contacts till I got to "Trish," and hit the big green button that read, "Call."

It rang. Rang again. My heart jogged, and it seemed absurd to be afraid to talk to my sister, of all people, but here I was. It connected midway through the third ring, but nobody said, "Hello."

"Trisha?"

"Yeah," she said. More than anything, she sounded exhausted. We just sat like that for a minute, her silence a slow-moving glacier, and my breathing getting ever more panicked.

"You called me," I said.

"Yeah. I can't remember why."

"It was less than an hour ago," I said.

"I guess I thought you might have something to say for yourself."

"I don't, I guess. I'm sorry. I didn't mean to hurt you."

"I guess this was revenge or something? For Nick?"

"No," I said.

"Then what *was* it about?"

"I...."

"Never mind. I don't want to know." She took a deep breath. "Look, Nate, you're moving away, right?"

"I ... yeah. I think so," I said.

"It doesn't matter. Whatever you end up doing in your life, I don't want to see you. I don't want to have anything to do with you. Mom knows this, too, and she's okay with it."

"What do you mean? She doesn't want to see me either?" I said.

"You'll have to ask her. I just know that our family, such as it was, is basically over as far as I'm concerned. I don't want to see you, and Mom is going to do what she has to do to make sure that I don't ever again, okay?"

"Okay," I said. I was chilled and sick. *She's saying this to hurt me*, I thought. Maybe, maybe.

"I need to know one thing, though." She paused. Pain was

creeping into her voice now. "I need to know if you're still having sex with him. I just ... I don't want to know anything more than that. Just ... are you?"

I imagined her in her house last night, tossing and turning with anger and hurt while Joey and I laid together in his car, fucking, snuggling. Finally summoning Joey in the morning when she couldn't take it anymore. I was as sure she had asked him the same question as I was sure that he'd lied about it.

I wanted to lie, too. Every part of my body and psyche screamed for me not to say it. But she was asking, and if there was anything to salvage here, any scrap of myself as a good person and a good brother, this was what I had to do.

"We did last night," I said.

She made a sound—a tortured *oof*—a sound like I'd reached inside of her, grabbed hold of her guts, and twisted them in my fist.

"Do not call me," she said and hung up. I looked at the phone, "Call Ended" blinking on the screen for a moment before it went black.

I cancelled my ticket to New York that afternoon. I can't say it was a rational decision.

"Wouldn't it be a good idea to get away?" Randy suggested. "Get some distance from it all?"

I knew he was right, but I didn't care. I wanted to stay in Groom, for now and maybe for the rest of my life, and if all my dreams went to shit, well, maybe that was what I deserved.

23

August turned into September. I stayed at Randy's. Worked a lot. He made me a manager and gave me a raise.

Then one day he got this idea. It was early evening—our busiest time, when the men needed their post-work, pre-family-time blowjobs (getting or giving, as you please). I'd just finished a new chalk mural, this one touting our DVD sale by featuring a horny Tasmanian Devil, arms loaded with DVDs and tongue hanging out of his mouth, a line of people exiting the store behind him—buxom beauties carrying dildos and whips. I managed to feature a lot of the merchandise in the store, and Randy was totally into it.

Randy and I were having a cigarette out in front while Sara, the new girl, tried to sell some dildos to a woman I'd sat next to in church when I was five. Sara was fresh out of high school, had dyed-blue hair, two boyfriends and a girlfriend. Randy and I loved her. Even with the extra help, I was working nearly every day, mostly to distract myself. Randy loved it because it gave him time to entertain whatever ridiculous notions popped into his head.

"It occurred to me last night that I can do more with this place than just, you know, create a fucking sale, or put paper towels in the booths. I've got money, more money than I know what to do with. The store is paid for. My property taxes don't amount to much. Dom had a lot of medical bills at the end, but his life insurance took care of all that. Plus, my mom left me with a nice chunk of cash when she died, and I haven't done anything with it. The point is: I don't care if this store makes money anymore." He turned to me. He had an excited look in his eyes that made him look younger. "I know what it is now: a place where people congregate. It's like a church, or a bar."

"A church, Randy? Really? I mean, they congregate all right, but it's hidden. It's in the shadows," I said.

"Exactly," he said, pointing his finger at me. "So what if we built a social area into the store? I mean, why not? What I'm thinking is that we could open up the entrance to the arcade. Have a couch or two. Some coffee. Make an area that wouldn't necessarily be visible to the rest of the store, but would still be accessible."

"People would fuck on that couch," I said.

"Not if it was visible enough. And maybe nobody would use it. But then maybe they would."

"It's bananas," I said.

"Exactly," Randy said, stamping on his cigarette butt. "I'm through with rational thinking. These jagweeds aren't gonna be buying DVDs forever once they figure out they can get everything for free on the Internet. The arcade is our bread and butter, always has been. We don't brighten it up so much as make one little area that's more than just a cubbyhole to suck cock in."

"What if it keeps people away? The closeted ones—they don't want it to be more social back there. They want to get in, get off, and get out," I said.

"Fuck 'em," Randy said.

"What if it makes it more visible to ... the authorities, I

228

guess."

"Some things are worth the risk," he said.

"I'm all for it," I said.

"I knew you would be." He clapped me on the shoulder, tousled my hair.

I should mention that, a week after my sister had called me and I'd decided to stay in Groom for a while, Randy and I had gotten drunk at the Silver Tongued Devil and wound up making out in his car. I think we both felt stupid about it in the morning, but it seemed like something that needed to happen. Now, we were on solid footing as friends. It was a different kind of thing for me, a type of relationship I'd never had with an older guy, and even though I think Randy would've done more with me, I wasn't sure about it myself and I didn't want to fuck anything up.

Sara came outside. "It's a total dick bonanza in there," she said. She bummed a cigarette off Randy. "Mural finished?"

"Yep," I said.

"I wish I could draw," she said, walking around it. "You're lucky."

I did feel lucky, in some ways. My dad had given me this ambition to become an artist, and as much as it tortured me, it also motivated me. That satisfaction of making something was so strong.

That was another thing that had happened in the days since I stopped talking to my family and Joey. I found that I didn't want to talk to anybody about what happened, not even Randy so much. I even let my phone plan expire.

I started drawing a lot. At first it was just to fill up spare time. I found this huge pad of paper in Randy's attic and I started doing these large, abstract designs. They didn't matter to me, so I had fun with them, and once I started having fun, I realized that I actually *wanted* to draw, and that I liked what I was producing.

Then I found a stack of stretched blank canvases at the thrift store on Market Street, so I bought them. I splurged and bought some paint when Randy drove us out to the mall one afternoon. I made myself a studio space in his guest room as soon as I got home, then I tried painting one of the drawings I'd done. Five hours later, it was well into the next morning, and I'd barely looked up from the canvas. I'd gotten into that zone, total concentration and focus, and it felt so good.

Randy saw it the next morning and said he loved it, so I offered to give it to him.

"Save it for a show," he said, but I insisted, mainly because it gave me a reason to put it away and start on another one.

By the time I had six paintings finished and three more in progress, Randy's guest room was beginning to look like Pollack had had a seizure in it. I knew it was time to find my own place. Just a month ago the idea of getting an apartment in Groom would have seemed like the concession to end all concessions, a tomb for my dreams: professional porn store worker and full-time Groom resident, Nate Audley.

But I was past that. I had enough money saved that I wouldn't be dipping into my savings. Plus, this was Groom and apartments were cheap as shit.

And maybe if I was being honest with myself, I knew that one of the reasons I was sticking around was because what had happened with my family felt like unfinished business. That was the weirdest thing: One of the reasons I put down roots in Groom was because New York felt closer than ever. For the first time in maybe ever, I felt totally in the moment, completely in possession of myself.

I found an apartment on Main Street. It was little and not real clean, but it had a kitchen and old hardwood floors with an inch of varnish on them that stunk up the whole place. There was a skylight, and I set up my easel (made from the cardboard boxes the dildos came in) underneath it. Randy donated a rollaway bed, which Sara helped me move. We actually carried the damn thing from Randy's house three blocks away and up the stairs to my place.

"Dude, this place is the shit," she said, walking around. It was all pretty makeshift, but I loved it. I had a closet without a door, so it was just an open space with some wire hangers holding up my admittedly limited wardrobe. I put a sheet on the bed, but it wasn't the right size, so two of its elastic-bunched corners were brushing the floor. My little kitchen was furnished with thrift store junk. The thrift store was right downstairs, next to a pizza shop where I got most my dinners. But when pizza got old, I bought a cookbook at the thrift store and started teaching myself to cook

Seeing Sara admire it made me realize that it looked like a real artist's place. And hell, maybe I was a real artist. I was certainly producing like one, and while I had no idea if my stuff was good or bad, it almost didn't matter. I was happy. It reminded me of what it had felt like to draw with Nick in his attic in high school—just creating for the sake of creating and not worrying about where it was going.

By mid-October, I had over a dozen finished paintings, and they kept getting more intricate. I had enough money saved, and I was working more than I wanted to. I needed more time for art. So, I went to Randy one day.

We were outside. It was getting cooler. Randy's construction guy was inside, knocking down one of the arcade walls. It was a total mess in there. But it was fun having the construction guy around because he was straight and apparently an old friend of Randy's, and he was getting an eyeful of the place. He was a big strapping redheaded guy, and we all had a crush on him.

Randy sensed what I was going to ask him for before I said a word.

"C'mon, Nate, don't do this to me," Randy said.

"What do you mean? Sara is totally cool with picking up more shifts. She wants hours. I need more time to work on my art. Please, Randy? You know how important it is to me."

He relented eventually. There was in Randy some need that I fulfilled, a need to dote or mentor. I guess I felt like his son sometimes.

It was getting dark, and it was early, the late-October sun casting a deep orange glow over the parking lot as Randy puffed his cigarette. Sara had the night shift. I knew that Randy liked spending time with her like I did. She was young and kinky and very into the idea of being a porn store employee. She just fit.

"So, when are you gonna tell me more about your construction guy?" I said, changing the subject.

"That's Jim," Randy said.

"Is he gonna cruise the booths?"

"Nah. He's never been the anonymous type. He's like you, I guess. Needs that 'emotional connection' or whatever," he said, rolling his eyes.

"Believe me, I wish I didn't. Things seem infinitely less complicated back there," I said.

Randy shuffled his feet. "So, you haven't talked to them at all? Your mom or your sister?"

"No," I said. "I'm actually surprised I haven't run into either of them." What I didn't say was that I went out of my way to avoid them. I never walked past the bank where my sister worked, if I could avoid it.

"I know you probably don't want to hear this," Randy said, "but maybe it would be a good idea to talk to them. For their sake, or yours? They might be wondering where you are, and they don't have any way to find you."

It was true: I still didn't have a phone, and it was driving Randy and Sara crazy because they couldn't get a hold of me unless they came to my apartment, where I pretty much always was.

"I'm sure they don't want to hear from me," I said.

"Okay. I don't mean to guilt you into talking to them."

"It's okay. I mean, I know I'm not ready to face my mom. It's weird, like what I did was just an excuse to get distance from her, even though I spent the last four years over an hour away. I feel like I finally cut the cord."

Jim the construction guy came out. He slapped Randy on the ass and gave me a wink. "That porn arcade is just the damnedest thing," he said, lighting up a cigarette.

Larry followed. He'd been hovering around Jim all night. The four of us stood out there on the highway, chatting. A car honked as it went past and someone shouted from the window, "Perverts!"

Larry stepped forward, put his hand in the air, and bowed.

24

I thought about Joey, but not a lot. Mostly I wondered if he and my sister were still together, if she'd tried to make it work. Part of me hoped that they had: for her sake, and 'cause it would minimize the damage I'd done. But—and this is insanely hypocritical, I know—I didn't know if I could respect Trisha if she chose to stay with him.

More than once I thought about him while I jacked off, but my sex drive had veered off a cliff. I went through almost all of October without jacking off, which was odd for me.

Then, one night—my night off work—I saw him. It was a typical day. I slept all morning, then heated up spinach lasagna for lunch. Then I started painting. I had music going—my old iPod connected to a pair of beat-up computer speakers from the Goodwill. I'd stretched five new canvases the day before, and I started on a blank one. Well, first I stared at it for a good half hour. It was always the hardest, getting started.

Anyway, this one got interesting quickly, and when I finally looked up, it was around 11:00 p.m.. I was starving, and I was out of lasagna. I threw a jacket over my paint-streaked T-shirt (my jeans were worse) and headed out of the house.

I walked to the gas station on the corner. I had this moment where I was aware of how good I felt. I knew exactly what I wanted to do when I got home. It was just a matter of feeding myself to make it happen. I poured a big cup of coffee into a Styrofoam cup and used the touchscreen to order a chicken salad sandwich. They were closing in a half hour, and the guy behind the counter sighed in annoyance when my order beeped through.

Somebody tapped my shoulder. I turned around, and there was Joey.

"Hey," he said.

He looked different. He was wearing more clothes than usual: a tight ribbed thermal shirt that showed off his pecs and nubby nipples, a pair of track pants, the ones that buttoned down the sides of the legs.

"How you been? Long time no see," he said, putting his hands into the pockets of his track pants, which pushed them downward. This revealed a strip of his tight white stomach. His happy trail had grown back.

I said I was good and exchanged the usual pleasantries while trying to ignore how awkward it was.

He glanced around the store as we talked, which was buzzing with late-night traffic. "I thought maybe you moved," he said.

"Still here," I said. "Still working at the porn store. But I got my own place."

"You did?" he said, perking up, and god help me if I didn't perk up a little myself.

"Yeah," I said. "How about you?"

"I'm staying at Bev's," he said, gesturing toward the window of the store. Bev was standing out there. My eyes met his. "Been there a couple weeks," Joey added, moving so that he was between me and the window. "So ... what are you doing later?"

He had a party to go to with Bev, and needed an hour or so to get in and get out. I told him where my apartment was. He knew the building. I got my sandwich and beverage and went home to eat it, but I was so anxious that I wasn't hungry anymore.

I wanted it. I didn't want it. I thought I might not answer the door when he came. But then I would get so hard thinking about what might happen.

When he finally came knocking at 2:00 a.m., with a bottle of wine in his hand, I let him in.

We were making out before we even got to my apartment door, right there in the stairwell. I had my hand down his pants and he had his hand down mine, but, I noticed, neither of us were getting hard, and there was something desperate and anxious about it. I finally broke it off, and we went upstairs and cracked open the wine, which we drank out of coffee mugs.

"Nice place," Joey said, glancing around.

"Thanks," I said and sat next to him on my bed.

"These paintings, did you do them?"

"Yeah," I said, laughing at him. I mean, half of them were unfinished, and the place was swarmed with art supplies. It was pretty obvious.

"I didn't know you could paint."

"Yeah, I've been getting into it lately."

We drank our wine. Why was this so awkward? In the past, all we would've talked about was sex—him wanting my cock, me wanting his. I started to feel hopeless, stuck with this douchebag in my apartment when all I wanted to do was work.

I decided to try. I got down on my knees in front of him

and went for his cock, sucked it for a good five minutes, and he only ever managed to get it half-hard. I wasn't hard either, but it was like I couldn't stop. Finally, he took my head out of his lap.

"Man, I'm drunk," he said—as an excuse, I guess.

"Sorry," I said, though I wasn't sorry about anything. I sat next to him and filled our mugs again. "So, have you been working on anything?"

"Just this bookshelf at my studio. I'm making it for your sister," he said.

"The same bookshelf?" I said and felt my eyes narrow.

"Yeah. Have you talked to her lately?"

"No. Not since that day we parked up on Derry Lane."

"She kicked me out that morning," he said.

"She asked me if we'd been together that night and I told her," I said.

"Oh, that's why," he said.

"Don't act like I ruined it for you, Joey."

He looked at me, seemed annoyed.

I said, "Should I have lied? How long do you think we could've kept that up?"

"I don't know," he said. "She didn't even let me get my stuff, just put it out into the yard. Some of it was wet and shit. I tried to talk to her the next few nights, but then she called the cops on me. It was so fucked up."

I managed not to roll my eyes. *I'm over this*, I thought. *We're both over this.*

"She asked me when it started," he said.

"What did you say?"

"I told her we'd only been doing it a couple weeks," he said, shrugging.

"She's too smart to believe that." I set down my mug. It was like a frigid breeze had wafted through the apartment and right between us. Neither of us knew what to do. I wanted it to be like it was, but it wasn't.

I got up. So did Joey.

"I guess I better get home," he said.

"Well, thanks for stopping by." I let him out. We didn't even shake hands. I poured the rest of the wine down my chipped ceramic sink, tossed the bottle into the trash. I thought of my stigma against the back room of the porn store, all those anonymous encounters. Had it been any different with Joey? It felt like it at the time, but we'd still wound up strangers.

I was ashamed. I'd bought into something, some image, some fantasy, and in an instant it had vanished, like the sun had burned off the fog and revealed a dead desert.

Jim the construction guy was almost finished with our arcade expansion, what Randy and Sara and I were calling our "gracious drawing room." Basically, he'd uninstalled one of the booths and knocked down part of the outside wall to create a sitting area, which was set back from the store, just inside the arcade. Randy put in a leather sofa, a wing-backed chair, and a table with a lamp on it. We put air fresheners in there to distract from the arcade smell with its unique mélange of urine, come, and pine-scented cleaner. What was great about it was that we could hang out in there, but still keep an eye on the store, so we would work and hang out at the same time.

Since Sara was always back there, Randy looked up the supposed state law saying that women weren't allowed in jack-off arcades and couldn't find one. Apparently it was just a policy from the old store owners to discourage prostitution or something. We decided we'd let women back there if they wanted to go. Only a few did. "They'll start coming once word gets out that we're hetero-friendly," Sara said.

"We'll cross that bridge when we come to it," Randy said.

In fact, we'd been scheming on how to make the store more gay-friendly. Randy ordered some leather-guy stuff, and we made a section for it—cock straps, harnesses, nipple clamps. I sold a Tom-of-Finland-style leather cap to a guy who'd been my Sunday school teacher. He didn't remember me, and I wasn't sure he understood what he was buying.

We did another display that was an ode to the female orgasm, with facts about vibrators through the ages and information about places where dildos were illegal.

Jim was such a hot ginger daddy, and while Randy claimed he was bisexual, I never saw him getting into anything. He was flirty, and we liked teasing him, like the day we got him to try to scope Lloyd's legendary cock. He said he couldn't see it 'cause it was down somebody's throat.

Sara grabbed me one night when we were switching shifts. "There's a film festival in Brooklyn that my friend is going to have a movie in. I might go for a few days. Are you interested?"

"Absolutely," I said, just like that.

Here is where I reveal my pathetic secret: I'd never even

visited New York at that point. We bought bus tickets and found a place to stay over Thanksgiving weekend, which was perfect. There were holidays coming up, and at least I wouldn't have to think about what I was doing for this one.

25

Then I finally ran into Trish. Well, "ran into" isn't really accurate. She came to find me.

I was at work. Randy and Larry were hanging out in the gracious drawing room. Larry had essentially appointed himself mayor of the place, which was funny 'cause he'd originally been the most against it.

"Who wants to mingle with these people?" he'd said. "I see what I want, I get it, and I get out."

But I think he was taken with the cuteness of the space, and, more importantly, he could exercise his bountiful gift of gab. We had so much fun trying to get people to sit and hang out with us. A lot of them just wanted to disappear into the darkness, so it was funny to watch them react to it, this little living room in front of the porno booths. The really closeted ones would visibly recoil, especially if we had a nice group socializing there. Or they'd fasten their eyes to the floor, quicken their pace. These guys, some of whom had been getting blowjobs on the way home to their wives for years, knew the deal in the back room, how to cruise and get cruised. But an area to sit and talk in was something else. Randy actually got customer complaints about it, which he ignored.

"They'll suck cock back there no matter what we do to the place," he said. "We could slather the walls in pink glitter and hang stuffed unicorns from the ceilings, and they would *still* suck cock back there," he said.

I was behind the counter, smoothing and stacking the arcade coupons in groups of fifty, which was how we kept track of how many we sold. Randy kept a bottle of hand sanitizer behind the counter for moments just like this, and I was pumping some into my hand, getting ready to help whomever had just dinged the bell when I looked up and saw that it was my sister.

Her face, when we looked into each other's eyes, was blank, like an overload of emotions had short-circuited her nervous system. I imagine I looked the same, only more so because I hadn't been expecting to see her. Certainly not there.

Randy stepped over to greet her. "Can I help you find anything today?" he said.

"No, thanks," she said.

Randy looked at her, looked at me. He figured it out and retreated back to the parlor.

"Hey," I said. My heart was pounding.

She approached the counter. She looked different. She'd cut her hair. "Hey," she said. "I couldn't get a hold of you. It says your phone number is disconnected."

"Yeah, I let my plan expire," I said.

"Mom thought you moved," she said, glancing around the store. Randy had put these giant rubber dildos and fists right next to the counter just to make people laugh. I watched her eyes settle on one called "Sir Dick," and she looked away quickly, pulled her purse tighter around her shoulder. "She's all worried."

"I need to stop by and see her," I said.

"That's a good idea. She's driving me nuts, thinking you're, like, dead in an alley in New York City or something."

"Still here," I said.

She nodded. I could see the hurt in her eyes, the strength she was pulling on to make herself do this. "Look," she said, "would you be willing to get coffee with me? Tomorrow? Are you working?"

"No, I'm off," I said.

"I guess we could just meet at the diner? In the morning?"

"Like, what time?"

"Nine?"

"Could we make it ten?" I said.

"Yeah," she said.

I saw Randy and Larry poking their heads out to look. Trish followed my gaze, and they immediately, awkwardly, looked away.

"I'll see you then," she said. As she left the store, she looked around, seemed almost amused by it.

"The infamous sister," Larry said.

"She's gorgeous," Randy said.

"She really is. What a cute outfit," Larry said.

"Yeah, those pants...," Randy said.

"Really chic," Larry said.

"I guess I'm meeting her tomorrow for coffee," I said. They nodded at me.

Randy put his hand on my shoulder. "That's a good thing," he said.

Larry raised an eyebrow. "I wouldn't leave your coffee cup unattended around her, if I were you."

I woke around 6:00 a.m. and couldn't get back to sleep. I watched the clock until 9:30, entertaining escape plans like hitchhiking to California or committing suicide.

Finally, I headed to the diner with a book under my arm. I was reading it—well, reading one paragraph over and over and not comprehending a word—when Trisha walked in the door and sat across from me.

"I like your jacket," I said.

"Thanks. They gave me a raise at work, so I've been honing my shopping skills," she said, arranging her purse next to her on the seat. "I go with Mom. She's all about it."

"Is she okay?" I said.

"Yeah, fine. The same."

The waitress came. Trisha ordered a coffee. I ordered a donut to go with the coffee I already had. The coffee came, and Trisha stirred cream into it, the silence between us gathering tension like an electrical charge in a storm cloud. She kept taking quick glances at me, then her eyes would dash all over.

"Anything else?" the waitress said, and her cheery tone landed on us like laughter at a funeral.

"No, thanks," I said.

The waitress walked away.

"Look, Nate...," Trisha started. I braced myself. "I've thought a lot about it. I thought I might not be able to get past it, that I might not be able to be around you. Now I'm thinking, I don't know if that's realistic. Even though that's what I said."

I nodded.

245

"That's all I really wanted to say to you. That, you know, despite everything ... or anything that might happen ... we're still going to be brother and sister. Whether I like it or not." She sat back in the booth. "I don't know what that means. Things are weird now, and they'll probably have to be that way for a while."

"I know," I said. "I mean, I understand."

Her expression hardened. "There's shit I want to ask you, that I want to know. But I know I'm better off not asking," she said.

I could imagine. I imagined they were the same things I wanted to tell her, things I wanted to absolve myself of. How long we'd been doing it under her nose, where we'd done it, maybe even why.

"You should know that he's not living with me anymore. I don't want to have anything to do with him. And...." She took a deep breath. "I don't know what you two have...."

I wanted to say "nothing" because it felt like the truth, but I didn't because I wasn't sure if it was honest and, besides, she hadn't asked.

"I don't want to know. But I don't—*don't*—want to see him. I mean, not anywhere. But especially not around us, our family," she said.

"That's not a problem," I said.

Trisha looked at me. "I do want to say ... you were honest with me, when I asked you. I appreciated that."

It was gratitude, but it laid on me like sadness. There was this war going on inside her, I sensed, this impulse to protect me, to soften everything, to parent, even in a situation where

246

I'd betrayed her. And there was my impulse to push away from that, even when I wanted it.

"I'm sorry," I said. "For everything."

"Don't, Nate," she said, shaking her head and looking down at her coffee. "I don't doubt that you're being sincere, but ... just don't."

I nodded. We sat and drank our coffees. Eventually, something like relief set in. Relief that I hadn't lost my connection to my family, that I hadn't set myself completely adrift.

"Where are you staying?" she said.

"I got an apartment on Market Street."

"Really? Mom will be impressed. You should reach out to her. Especially since tomorrow is the anniversary."

I'd completely forgotten. The anniversary of Dad's death.

"Maybe give her a few days, though. For your own sake," she said. We both knew how she got around that time.

"I won't be around for Thanksgiving. I mean, not that we were supposed to do anything," I said.

"No, Mom asked. She wants to make a dinner."

"Well, I'm taking a trip." Trish didn't seem interested, so I didn't elaborate.

"You've been avoiding her for months. She's not gonna know the difference," she said and smiled. A small smile. "You're so gonna stick me with her for life, aren't you?" I looked at her, guiltily I'm sure. She just shrugged. "I don't mind. Spending time with her, I mean. She's funny, you know. More than we give her credit for. And she loves us."

"She's not a bad mom," I said.

"Right. Not always."

I wondered, did she appreciate that Mom had told her? I couldn't imagine how confusing that would be.

◆

I waited until the day before I left for NYC to see my mom. As the trip neared, I got excited about the actual prospect of living there and started doing some research. It was thrilling to realize that there really were options—people who needed roommates, coffee shops and stores that were hiring—once I really put my mind to examining them.

I was so happy in my little space in Groom was the thing. Sometimes I really did feel like moving to New York would be a folly. I had everything I needed. My paintings were getting ... if not better then at least more elaborate and interesting to me. But the plan was set in my mind and had been for some time. If I didn't go for it, I'd always wonder.

In Mom's backyard was a big pile of trash in which I recognized my dad's old desk. I knocked on the back door before I opened it.

"Donna?" she said from the kitchen.

"It's me, Mom."

"Oh." She was on the kitchen floor, going through the stuff in the bottom of the hutch. She glanced up at me hesitantly. I didn't want to think about what she saw now when she looked at me. "Hi, honey."

"Hi." I sat down at the table as she continued to reach into the bowels of the hutch, pulling out handfuls of Dad's old magazines, scraps of construction paper, stuff that had been there since I was a kid.

"Trisha said she saw you a couple of weeks ago," she said.

"Yeah. We got coffee."

"Well, I'm glad you two are talking," she said. She stopped rummaging, but still sat on the floor.

"Me, too," I said.

Finally, she stood, smoothed out her pants, and faced me.

I said, "I mean, I don't know how much we're talking, but we met up, and it was good."

Mom regarded me, swallowed. "You look older," she said.

"It's only been two months."

"I suppose so. You just look different. Maybe you cut your hair."

"Yeah, maybe." I hadn't. "What are you doing anyway?"

"Getting rid of old things. Your uncle is helping me. We've got that pile in the backyard. The basement is almost totally cleaned out."

"How's your health?"

"Well, I'm hanging in there." And she went on about her various medical adventures over the past couple of weeks. There was something comforting about it, listening to her talk about her problems. There was something maddening about it, too.

"I wanted to tell you, Mom, I don't know if you planned to have me around for Thanksgiving...."

"Trisha said you're going on a trip," she said.

"Yeah, I am."

"Well, okay. Nate...." There was a long, awkward pause.

249

"Are you still ... seeing him?"

"No," I said.

"Good," she said and went to the sink. She poured herself a glass of water.

"Mom, why did you tell her? I asked you not to tell her."

This came out with more anger than I'd anticipated. The anger was so potent, so belly deep, that it was undeniable, even as I tried to force it down and keep my tone measured. Why did I even think I had a right to be angry?

"I know," she said. "But I couldn't be sure that you would tell her." She was crying. It made me angry. What was so upsetting to her that she had to cry, in this situation? Besides her catching us, it barely involved her.

"I *told* you I was going to tell her," I said.

"But how would I know if you actually *would!*" She was really crying now.

I didn't want any of it. Didn't want to make my mother cry, didn't want to feel guilty about it, didn't want to resent her for it. I said, "I'm an adult, Mom. It was stupid, what I did, but how am I ever going to grow up if you don't trust me?"

"You don't act like an adult," she said. "You're just like your father in that respect."

"*Stop fucking saying that,*" I said, all but shouted it.

"Language!" she said.

"I have to go, Mom. I'll be back around Christmas."

She wiped her eye with her hand. "I'm sorry I'm such a terrible mother," she said.

"*I have to go,*" I said, and I left, and I felt relief.

250

26

I've seen Joey just once since then. It was a few months after I got back from New York with Sara, which had been a great time, even if I hadn't found my holy grail of a job with an apartment attached to it. We'd had a blast, giddy in the city, scurrying around like rats on the subways and streets from one thing to the next. That's the thing about New York—there's always something happening there. I'd been cooped up in Groom all summer, and Sara had lived in Groom her whole life. We feasted.

Christmas came around. I helped Randy decorate the store. We got a fake tree and hung dildos and condoms from it. He was still upset that I was moving, but he tried not to show it. In fact, he got downright encouraging.

"People move there all the time. There's no reason you can't do it, too," he said.

I appreciated it because he was the one reason I might have stayed. In fact, sometimes I *wanted* him to want me to stick around, but he was too good of a person not to support what I wanted.

Then, one day, Sara was working the register and I was in the back office doing payroll. I locked up the office and started through the back room. I saw Lloyd, gave him a nod and a smile, which he returned. Beyond him was a younger guy, hot guy, leaning against a booth, cruising. When I got closer, I realized it was Nick.

"Hey," I said. Nick's jaw dropped. I was totally thrown, so I just kept walking until I got into the light of the store.

"You see a ghost back there or something?" Sara said.

"No," I said, sidling up to the register. "Well, sort of...."

Then Nick strode out from the back and came up to me.

"Hey Nate," he said.

"Hey."

"Can you, uh, meet me outside for a minute?"

"Absolutely," I said. "I just have to run this report, and I'll be right out."

When I went outside, Nick was standing in the sunlight around the side of the store, smoking a cigarette. I awkwardly greeted him. Neither of us knew what to say.

"So," I said.

"I had no idea you, uh, worked here," Nick said.

"Yeah, I worked here all summer."

Nick nodded, looked down at the pavement. I could see how uncomfortable he was.

I said, "Look, Nick, I wouldn't say anything to anybody. I mean, it's none of my business."

"Okay," Nick said. He tossed his cigarette into the weeds and leaned against the wall. "It's okay. I've just ... this is actually only the second time I've ever been in here."

"Yeah?"

"Yeah. I came in once a couple years ago. Before I met Amy." He shuffled on his feet, looked up at me. "We broke up. Like, a few weeks ago."

"Oh. I'm sorry, man."

"Thanks," he said. "She moved. It sucked, but it wasn't,

252

like, the worst breakup I've ever had."

"Still," I said. A semi pulled into the lot. We watched it loudly go past us. "It's unfortunate that we haven't hung out more since I've been back."

"It's okay," he said. "I know things are different than they were in high school. I mean, it's no big deal."

"Yeah. But, honestly, I could've used a friend. Things got really fucked up this summer with my sister."

"Like how?"

"I'll tell you about it some other time," I said.

"Yeah, sure," he said.

The awkwardness had dissipated, and we were looking at each other with more ease. And then I had all these questions start to surface, like had he been back there just to jack off, or was he looking for something more? And if he was looking for something more, could I be the one to give it to him?

Did I even want that?

"I mean, things have always been weird," he said. "Ever since high school. I, uh ... I know I apologized to you back then for, you know, with your sister. Dating her or whatever."

"It's okay. It was a long time ago."

"Yeah, but, you know, it was Amy actually who said it. When I told her what you and I had done together in high school...."

"You told your ex-girlfriend about us?" I said.

"Yeah," he said, laughing. "Is that okay?"

"Well, sure, I guess. I'm just surprised," I said.

"Yeah, I told her everything. I mean, not everything about us, just ... everything." I nodded. "I guess she made me realize how that must have been for you back then. Like, how I was the only one who knew you were gay, and we had this thing and ... not that it was anything more than what it was...."

"Right," I said quickly. I had known, even then, that what we'd had wasn't romantic. Not that I hadn't fantasized that from time to time.

"But even still, you know, you trusted me. And I betrayed that. So, I'm sorry," he said.

I took a deep breath. It was amazing that, even after all this time, I hadn't realized I'd needed that explanation from Nick. That, of course, my sister hadn't betrayed me at all.

"Thanks, man," I said. Nick nodded. We smiled at each other. Fuck, he was sexy. And I guess the months of chastity I'd had since everything with Joey was catching up with me. "So," I said. "If you don't mind my asking, what did you come here for today?"

Nick chuckled, though he seemed chagrined by my forwardness. "Oh, you know...."

"I do," I said.

"It's not ideal, but, well, there are not a lot of options around here. You know, for something quick and easy."

"You could always call me."

"Could I?" Nick said.

"Yeah, of course you could," I said.

"Cool," Nick said, grinning. "Funny, I'm getting hard already." I looked down. He was. "So ... what time do you get done?"

254

I won't lie. It was still awkward when Nick came up to my place. But awkward in an exciting way. I mean, we both knew what he was there for. Still, we hung out for a bit. I showed him my place, showed him my paintings. He'd been working on some stuff of his own since the breakup, and he showed me pics on his phone. Then we were sitting beside each other on the bed, and I handed his phone back to him, and neither of us knew how to start.

"We used to always look at porn," I said.

"Yeah," Nick said. "I guess I don't really need it," he said, motioning down to his lap. He was wearing workout pants, and there was nice, thick tent pole propping them up in the front.

I reached for his leg and slid my hand up to it. "I forgot how big it is," I said.

"Yeah," Nick said, looking at me, and then he just leaned into me and we started kissing. That was a surprise, and it turned me on like crazy. He held onto my shoulders while we made out.

"Hope that's not weird," he said once we broke apart.

"Not at all. I just didn't expect it. We never did that back in the day," I said.

"Yeah. I like to kiss. It turns me on. You're a good kisser."

"You, too," I said.

"Let's see if you're still good at sucking cock," he said with a smirk.

"I'm better," I said.

He laughed, but the meaning was clear: He still wasn't interested in doing anything to me. And actually, I was relieved. As interesting as it would have been to have full-on sex with Nick, I didn't think I was ready to get into something all that serious or to have my mind fucked by yet another blurred-lines relationship with a straight guy.

So, I got on my knees between Nick's legs and helped him slide off his pants while he lifted off his shirt. Damn, he looked good—big and beefy, with that fat cock bobbing around, just waiting for my mouth. I tried to make good on my boast and spent a while working him up, licking up his hairy thighs, slurping on his nuts, kissing his stomach, and sucking on his nipples. Finally, I went down on him, resting the head of his cock against my tongue and opening wide to swallow him down to the root. Nick moaned gratefully, and I kept a steady rhythm and a tight pressure, working his cock with my mouth and bringing him right to the brink. Then I'd pull off and suck on his nuts or lick his body. We made out some more. I took out my cock to jack off while I sucked him. That was another thing I'd never done back in the day, like I'd been afraid it would freak him out, but he just smiled now when he saw.

I cupped his heavy balls in one hand while I stroked myself in the other. His balls started to scrunch up, and his breathing got all manic.

"Fuck, Nate, you're gonna make me do it. I'm gonna come. Oh fuck!" Then he pumped what felt like gallons of thick semen into my mouth. At the same time, I shot all over the side of my bed and the floor, and even got some on his socks. Not that he cared. He just rubbed it in with his fingers.

I thought I'd feel bad afterwards. Like I'd reverted. But instead I just felt satisfied and, well, happy. I'd had a fun sexual encounter and reconnected with an old friend. But the best part was that there wasn't any guilt associated with it. It was a neutralizing experience in that way—a reminder that I really could enjoy sex without sin.

◆

I went to Mom's for dinner on Christmas Day. It was awkward but good. Trisha and I both showed up late, and neither of us got the other a present, but that was normal for us. Mom got Trisha this insanely huge and heavy fireproof safe. The look on Trisha's face when she unwrapped it was priceless. I had no idea what my mom was thinking when she bought it, let alone how she got it into her house. Trisha and I struggled just to get it into her car afterwards.

Mom gave me a bunch of pots and pans, which was nice, but I had most of that stuff already. Before we left, though, she gave me something else.

"Just some stuff of your father's that I've been holding onto," she said and handed me a beat-up cardboard box. It was full of notebooks and journals.

I flipped through one as Trisha drove me back to my apartment. It was cool to see his handwriting, but it just described surface events like holidays, the weather, the news of the world. But there were interesting tidbits like, "Janet took the kids to her father's; quality time alone."

"What the fuck am I going to do with that thing?" Trisha

said, motioning to the safe sinking into the back seat.

"I'll help you take it up your driveway, if you want," I said.

"No, that's okay," Trisha quickly said.

We pulled up in front of my place and I tossed the notebook I was reading into the box.

"Will you let me read those when you're done?" she said.

"Yeah, definitely."

"It scares me, what might be in there, you know?" she said.

I knew what she meant. It was easier to keep him in my mind as he'd always been—barely there.

I smoked a joint when I got home and started rooting through my dad's old stuff again. There was a manila envelope against the side of the box, and inside was a key for a post-office box. I could guess which one. I wondered if Mom had put it in there or if it had been where Dad kept a spare.

At the bottom of the box were three fat, black-cloth covered notebooks. Unlike the other notebooks, they didn't look like they'd been used all that much. At first I thought they were blank, but I opened one, and it said in big letters on the top margin, "My Boss's Wife."

Two pages was all it took for me to realize that my dad had written a porno novel. It filled the other two notebooks as well—one continuous story that I read practically without looking up until it was finished.

It gave me a boner. A couple times. I'm not gonna lie.

"Did you know about it?" I asked my mom.

"Oh, for heaven's sake," she said. I'd approached the subject with caution. Read the whole thing over twice. Considered whether it was really worth talking about.

My Boss's Wife was about an office in the city. The protagonist was this young guy who—you guessed it—starts fucking his boss's wife. The funny thing was that the voice of the wife sounded, for better or weirder, a lot like my mom. Her character was reticent and squeamish, but when it came down to it, she was a freak, and the two of them have all sorts of adventures, with themselves and others.

"Well ... did you?" I said 'cause Mom was just sitting there on the phone. She seemed distracted. "What are you doing?"

"I'm watching the dryer spin."

"Why are you doing that?"

"Of course I knew," she said, changing the subject. "But I forgot all about it. Why'd you have to go and read that?"

"For fuck's sake, Mom—."

"Nathan!"

"I'm sorry, but you *gave* it to me. Of course I was going to read it. And, you know, it's not that bad," I said, and it was true. Yeah, it was porny and corny, but the characters were engaging, and there was some believable stuff about working in an office. Moreover, it was a *novel*, the only other one he'd written, as far as I knew.

"I barely remember a word," she said, but then she giggled. "Except for that scene on the rollercoaster," she said.

"He could tell a good story!"

"When he wanted to, I guess," she said.

"Right. When he wanted to," I said. "What if I tried to get it published?"

"Published? Do you think?" she said.

"Why not?" I said. I'd thought about it. Dad had a fan base,

259

small and cultish as it was. People would be fascinated that he wrote another novel, no matter its genre.

"Certainly nobody would want to publish *that*," she said, but I could hear something in her voice. She was tickled. It wouldn't take much convincing.

I was more cautious about mentioning it to my sister. It seemed too relevant. Did my whole family have to be so intimately involved in each other's sex lives? So, I just gave her the whole box and let her discover it for herself (along with the mailbox key—I figured she could check it if she wanted to). I dropped it off at her house—the first time I'd been there since the day I got caught. I didn't stay long and I didn't go past the kitchen. She seemed comfortable and happy. I spotted a guy's shirt draped across the back of her couch—button-down, not a wifebeater.

She called me a few days later. She'd found the novel, of course.

"It's abysmal," she said. "But I couldn't stop reading it."

"'Abysmal?'" I said, but I was smiling. "I mean, it's not high art. But neither was his other book."

"It's lively ... spunky—oh, god...."

"Never mind," I said, and we laughed

I found a reasonable place to crash in Brooklyn for at least a month. I figured it was now or never, and the day after New Year's, I bought my third bus ticket there, this time a one-way. I put in my two weeks, and Randy said I could stay with him if

I needed to come back. I hoped that wouldn't be the case, but it was relieving to have the option.

I went for a walk one late afternoon a couple days before I moved. The sun was low, and there were gritty dirt-flecked lumps of snow mounded on the sides of the street.

I was on South Spring Street, going past this house that had scaffolding on the side of it and lumber piled on the front porch. There was a maroon Cadillac parked in front.

I quickened my pace, then slowed. I wasn't sure if I wanted to see him or not. I was just past the house when he came out the side door. He had on tan Carhartt pants, and he was still wearing that damned wifebeater, even though it was winter. He had a cigarette hanging out of his mouth.

Joey. He glanced back to where a younger guy was following him. The guy was maybe still in high school. He was cute, dark-haired with a scruffy beard. Narrow waist, tight butt.

I averted my gaze, walked faster, but it was too late. I'd been spotted.

"Hey!" Joey called. He jogged toward me, smirking around his lit cigarette. "What's up, man?"

"Not too much," I said. "I'm moving."

"New York?" he said. The dark-haired guy was watching us. He shifted on his heels, looked at the ground, back at us.

"Yeah," I said.

"Cool," Joey said.

"You're working on this house?" I said.

"Yeah, we're redoing one of the bedrooms," he said. He followed my gaze back to the dark-haired guy, but he didn't

261

acknowledge him. Joey looked at me. He had this open gaze—open like a pit where you could dump your desires. He wanted me to do that. Maybe he wanted everybody to. It was the kind of person he was.

But what kind of person was I? I didn't feel any desire for him where, a few months before, I'd been ravenous. Now I just noticed the dull whiteness of his skin in the winter light, the smell of him, which triggered something fleeting and tinged with anxiety. Was I the type of person who got off on sneaking around, who'd been attracted to somebody just 'cause it was transgressive?

At the end of my dad's porno book, the guy fucking his boss's wife gets fired and buys a farm. He lives alone and relishes the seclusion.

Me, I was going to the city. I wasn't going to keep myself in the basement like my dad had. I liked my family too much. I liked myself too much.

"Well," I said. "I'll see ya."

"Yeah, man," he said, glancing past me at something up the street. I turned to look, but there wasn't anything there. Joey gave me one last look, as open as the sky, and jogged back toward the dark-haired guy. They walked to the slanted basement door and Joey grabbed the handle, hauled it open. He put his hand on the young man's lower back and led him down the stairs, their bodies disappearing foot by foot as they went underground.

THE END

Author Bio

Natty Soltesz has been writing gay smut with a literary bend since 2000. His first two books (*Backwoods* from Rebel Satori Press and *College Dive Bar, 1 A.M.* from Go Deeper Press) were Lambda Literary Award finalists. In 2009 he co-wrote a porno movie called *Dad Takes a Fishing Trip*. You may have jerked off to his work in defunct rags like *Freshmen* and *Mandate,* in books like *Best Gay Romance 2013,* and on free story sites like The Nifty Erotic Stories Archive. He lives in Pittsburgh and posts new stories regularly on his Patreon: www.patreon.com/nattysoltesz

Lightning Source UK Ltd.
Milton Keynes UK
UKHW041859060223
416533UK00006B/406

9 781608 641673